D0033011

MIGHTY MORPHIN
POWER RANGERS
FISH in TROUBLED WATER

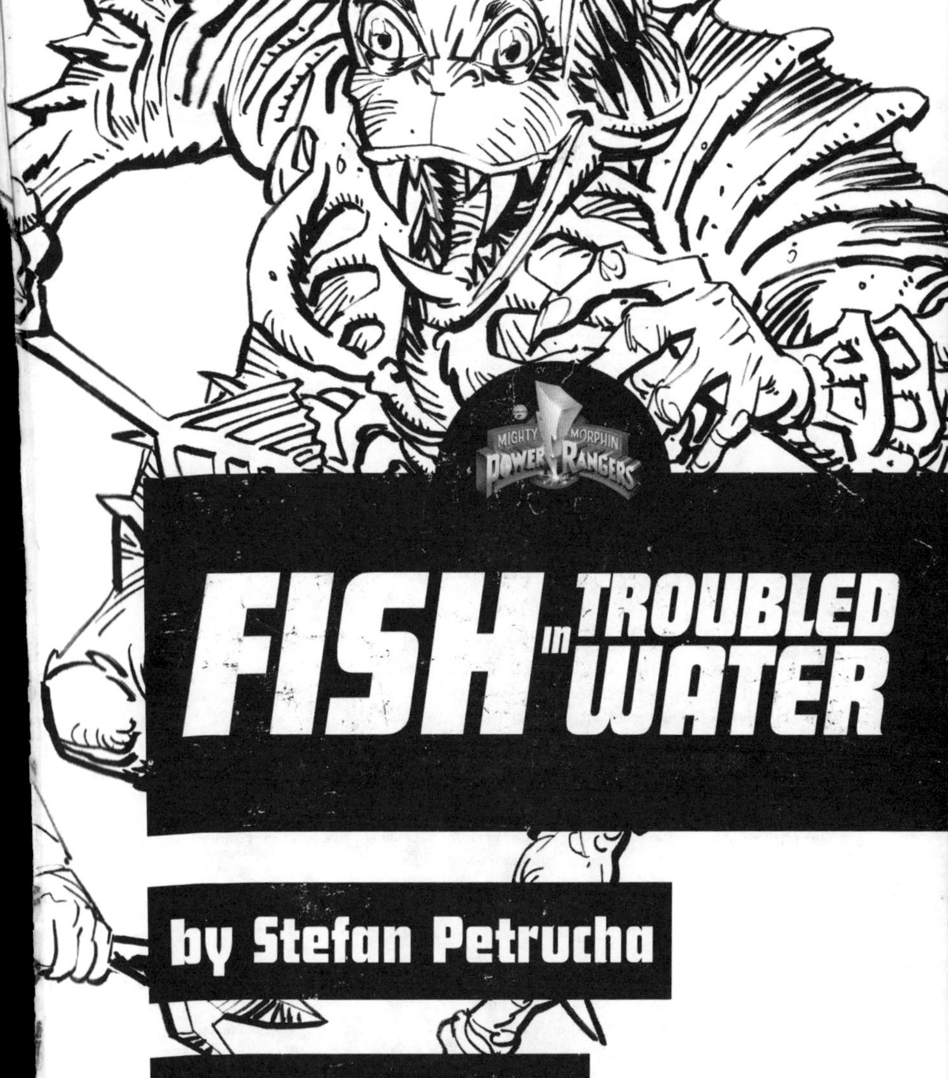

FISH in TROUBLED WATER

by Stefan Petrucha

Penguin Young Readers Licenses
An Imprint of Penguin Random House

PENGUIN YOUNG READERS LICENSES
An Imprint of Penguin Random House LLC

 Published by Penguin Young Readers Licenses, an imprint of Penguin Random House LLC, 345 Hudson Street, New York, New York 10014.
Printed in the USA.

Cover illustration by Dan Panosian

ISBN 9781524783822 10 9 8 7 6 5 4 3 2 1

Chapter 1

Despite all the flashing lights along the Command Center's computer panels, Billy Cranston, the sandy-haired Blue Ranger, remained completely focused on his work. The wrist-communicators he was trying to adjust were terribly important.

And he should know—he'd invented them!

The communicators not only allowed the five Mighty Morphin Power Rangers to contact one another at any time, but they also linked them to the Command Center's teleporter. That way, they could fight any monstrous attacks from the evil witch Rita Repulsa and her minions on a moment's notice, anywhere on Earth. Without the communicators, they'd have to wait for Zordon's robotic assistant, Alpha 5, to operate the teleporter for them.

Billy's invention had worked reliably until that morning, when a large storm began on the surface of the sun. Solar storms were common, but the flares they produced interfered with everything from radio signals to auto engines to Internet transmissions. Now they prevented the communicators from working. The storm would pass, sooner or later. In the meantime, Billy hoped he could get them up and running, in case there was an emergency.

So far, it wasn't looking good.

Much as his fellow Power Rangers wanted to get back to Angel Grove and enjoy some rare downtime, they knew not to hover while Billy worked. Alpha 5, who looked like a human except for his saucerlike head, was incredibly curious about anything humans did. The robot couldn't keep from asking questions.

"Why are you boosting the frequency instead of checking the circuits, Billy?" Alpha 5 asked.

Billy usually didn't mind. "I checked them before we got here," he answered.

Zordon, their guide and mentor, spoke up. "Alpha 5, let's let Billy concentrate while you work on tracking the solar flares. A solar storm of this magnitude could interfere with the teleporter itself! If he can figure out a way around that, it could be crucial in case of an attack!"

Billy knew the wise sage himself would love to do

more. After all, Zordon had fought Rita Repulsa ten thousand years ago, sealing her and her evil minions in a space Dumpster on the moon. Unfortunately, a last-ditch spell from the wicked witch had trapped Zordon in a time warp. With Rita free again, Zordon had to direct the battle from a special energy tube that maintained his delicate connection to this dimension and allowed him to communicate with the Power Rangers.

The tube also made him look like a big floating head. But his words, and his wisdom, were vital.

Billy's technical wizardry seemed like magic to some, but it was really just science. While he was good at it, there was only so much he could do. After two hours, he was about to call it quits when his phone alarm beeped, reminding him of another important responsibility.

Wiping his hands, he took a plastic bottle labeled FOOD from his pocket and sprinkled a few dried flakes into a small bowl he'd left on the Command Center workbench.

The goldfish inside munched away.

Alpha 5 turned his metal head. "You're taking a break to feed your pet?" he asked.

As he answered, Billy studied the fish. "Goo Fish

Junior isn't just a pet. He's part of an experiment."

Surprised to hear the name he'd given his fish, the other Power Rangers immediately stopped what they were doing. Kimberly Ann Hart, the Pink Ranger, froze in mid stretch and asked the question they were all thinking: "Isn't Goo Fish the name of a monster we fought?"

Billy nodded. "Yes. Specifically, it's the monster Goldar summoned when Rita Repulsa heard about my ichthyophobia."

Kimberly, Jason, and Zack looked at one another, puzzled.

Trini Kwan, the Yellow Ranger, completed the martial arts maneuver she'd been practicing and explained, "Fear of fish."

She was used to translating Billy's bigger words for the others.

Screwing the cap back on the bottle, Billy faced his friends. "It's thanks to that battle that I got over my fear and can work with fish. So Goo Fish Junior seemed appropriate," he said.

Alpha 5 leaned in for a closer look at the bowl. "An experiment?" he asked.

Billy adjusted his glasses and shrugged. "I've been

so focused on the communicators, I forgot to mention that I've been selected to spend a week, starting tomorrow, with thirty other high-school students at the Marine Island Research Center. We'll get to use the best scientific equipment in the world to work on our own special projects."

The others clapped and hooted. Alpha 5 spun happily in a circle.

Zack Taylor, the bighearted Black Ranger, slapped Billy on the shoulder. "Wow! Good for you, man!" he said.

Jason Lee Scott, the Red Ranger and their team leader, asked, "So, what's your experiment?"

Billy grinned proudly. "Using electroencephalography to image the brain waves of *Carassius auratus* for interspecies communication," he announced.

Jason, Zack, and Kimberly nodded. Then they looked to Trini.

"It's a way to get goldfish and people to talk to each other by reading their brain waves," she explained.

"Fantastic!" Kimberly said.

"Hey, that's what Trini does for you!" Zack joked.

Billy laughed along with them. Much as he loved his friends, he had to admit there were times he wished he didn't need any translator.

"I hate to step on your good news, Billy," Jason said, "but is there any hope for the communicators?"

Billy shook his head and began handing back the devices. "I've done everything I can, but until the storm passes, our contact with one another will be bad to none. In 1859 the biggest solar storm on record, called the Carrington Event, peaked for only a few days, so this should pass soon." He looked up at the sage's benevolent face. "Zordon, do you think I should cancel?"

"Your selflessness is appreciated, Billy," Zordon said. "But I'm confident Rita is still licking her wounds from her last battle with the Power Rangers. Your work on fish communication will help advance humanity's connection to the seas, and that is just as important."

Even Jason, who was the most serious about the Rangers, agreed. "I'm sure we can manage for a few days," he said.

"If we had to, we could walk!" Zack added.

Appreciating the support, Billy looked at Goo Fish Junior. "Guess we're going on a trip, little guy. What do you think of that? Hey, maybe soon I can actually ask you, and you'll be able to answer me!"

Goo Fish Junior only bubbled in response.

Chapter 2

In the ancient, multi-towered Moon Palace, 238,900 miles away, Rita Repulsa, the evil witch who wanted to dominate the galaxy, was very angry. She stomped around the workshop set aside for her monster-making minion Finster. Whenever she whirled, her flowing gown and crescent-moon-tipped wand sent alchemical potions, supplies, and notebooks flying. Finster, a short, furry, pointy-eared alien inventor, raced about behind her, catching his tumbling things when he could.

I have to wonder, Finster thought, *if she's doing all this damage on purpose!*

He knew better than to ask, though.

Finster had been loyally serving Rita for ages and still faithfully believed in her evil dreams. Ever since some unwitting astronauts from Earth released them from the cramped space Dumpster Zordon had trapped them in, they'd lived there in the Moon

Palace. There'd been good times and bad—mostly bad, thanks to the Power Rangers.

Today, though, Rita was in a particularly lousy mood.

"I'm sick of it, Finster! Sick of losing!" she shrieked. "I mean, how am I supposed to dominate an entire galaxy if I can't beat five putrid power punks? So what if my worst enemy, Zordon, helps them out? There's not much he can do, trapped in that time warp!"

When Finster didn't answer fast enough, she gave the biggest thing in the workshop, his Monster-Matic, a kick. Finster winced as if he'd been kicked himself. The Monster-Matic was his greatest invention. It allowed him to create everything from the faceless Putty Patrol to all manner of monsters, using his special clay.

Rita had a point, though. To date, they'd all been defeated by the Power Rangers.

Angry, she shook her wand at him and said, "You and this contraption better come up with something new and powerful that will take Zordon's ridiculous Rangers out once and for all!"

Like any good evil queen, Rita tended to be extreme. She was either laughing hysterically or getting enraged. Sometimes it was very hard for

Finster to tell which was coming next. It did keep Finster and her other minions, Goldar, Squatt, and Baboo, on their toes, though.

She waited for a response. Finster knew he had to say *something*, but all the drama left him mumbling.

"Well, your wickedness," he said softly. "I do have this idea I've been working on."

She wheeled toward him so fast that her dual-horned hairdo tipped over and nearly threw her off balance. Crouching like a stalking tigress, she pointed at her ear. "What'd you say? Speak up!"

Finster cleared his throat. "I said, I have an idea."

She rubbed her hands together. "An idea? Is it a new monster? An even bigger monster?" she asked excitedly. "A *monster*-size monster? I like it already!"

"Not exactly, my queen. It's a . . . device," Finster said. Instead of describing a terrifying creature, he held up a small rectangular gadget. It was full of buttons and lights. It looked so harmless, a human might mistake it for a TV remote.

Seeing it, her face dropped.

"I call it the Enhancifier," Finster said hopefully.

She grabbed it and turned it over. Then she made a face.

"The what? The fancy-liar? The pants-on-fire?" she asked.

"Enhancifier, your dreadfulness," he said. "With it, I can take any living creature, meld it with a preselected monster clay, and quintuple its power."

From the puzzled look on her face, Finster realized she didn't know the word.

"It's like double, only . . . more. Err . . . twice more and add one, your malevolence," Finster explained.

She stiffened. "Math?" she asked, insulted. "You want me to do math? Oh, just listening to you is giving me a headache! Baboo makes the gadgets; you stick to your clay!"

She threw the Enhancifier into the air.

Finster gasped then caught it. "But, your nastiness—" he said.

"No!" she said, cutting him off. "I've had enough of your big words and fancy arithmetic! I'm going to take a nap!"

As she stormed off, Finster started moping. Yes, of course his clay and the Monster-Matic were wonderful, but he knew he was also every bit as good with gadgets as that silly cross between a monkey and a bat, Baboo. Pouting, he started to clean up the mess

Rita had made in his workshop.

Why, even Rita herself says she only keeps Baboo around so there'll be someone to blame when something goes wrong! Finster thought. *And I* know *the Enhancifier is a perfectly good idea. If only I could get her terrible-ness to pay attention long enough to understand!*

Then, as if to prove to himself that he was an excellent inventor, he came up with a new idea.

I've got it! he thought. *I can use the Enhancifier to create something Rita* does *understand—that new, monstrous monster she wants, a great brute that's certain to squash the Power Rangers. All I need is the right animal. Then she'll see what I mean!*

Determined, Finster tiptoed out of his workshop. After making sure the wicked queen had indeed gone to sleep, he crept onto the observation balcony on the upper floor of the palace. There he found Rita's extreme long-range telescope and aimed it toward the distant blue-green Earth.

"There are so many different kinds of animals down there," he mused. "What sort would impress Rita the most? It has to be large and powerful to begin with, so my Enhancifier can make it even stronger. The humans keep some large animals in zoos, like elephants, but I want something even more spectacular."

And then he saw it, just off the California coast, in the Pacific Ocean: the Marine Island Research Center. It was the perfect place to begin his search.

"Whales, megasharks, giant squids!" he squealed. "There are plenty of powerful, frightening creatures out there!"

Chapter 3

The next morning the solar storm had gotten so bad, Zordon warned that, aside from Billy, the others should stick together since the communicators would be ineffective. But the solar flares didn't make the weather in Angel Grove any less sunny and beautiful. His notes and belongings packed, Billy said goodbye to his fellow Power Rangers and boarded a sleek water shuttle for the journey to the research center.

As the shuttle pulled out from the dock, they all waved. Trini called out, "Don't be afraid to make new friends!"

Billy waved back. She was only half kidding. He tended to be quiet around people he didn't know, and his fellow contest winners, from all over the country, would be strangers. But he could worry about that when he got there. In the meantime, the ocean ride was so bumpy, he was plenty busy trying to keep Goo Fish Junior's bowl from spilling over.

Two hours later, when Billy finally stepped off the shuttle and had his first up-close look at the Marine Island Research Center, he realized it was worth being shaken up a little. The research center was bigger than it had seemed in the pictures and even more amazing than he'd imagined.

There was a beautiful mountain at the far end of the island, with freshwater falls and a large, peaceful palm-tree forest. Closer to the docks, there were state-of-the-art buildings where the world's top marine biologists studied the ocean and all its creatures. A plaza had open-air pools for smaller species, but the five-story, 150-foot-tall main building, where Billy and the other students would live and work, had more than ten huge tanks for the bigger specimens.

Not just specimens, Billy reminded himself. The living creatures the scientists studied there were called "guests" and treated that way. They were always returned, unharmed, to their ocean homes. Billy loved the care and respect the scientists showed. He thought even the environmentally conscious Trini would approve.

Carrying the fishbowl and his belongings, Billy followed the welcome signs. As he got closer to the entrance to the main building, he had to stop and marvel. A member of the *Pseudorca crassidens* species, the fourth-largest type of dolphin, was sweeping gracefully along on the other side of a clear Plexiglas wall that formed part of one of the gigantic tanks inside.

Looking down at another fellow "guest," Billy said, "Don't worry, Goo Fish Junior. Big isn't the same as important."

The registration table was just around the curved Plexiglas. Seeing all the teens gathered there, Billy gulped. He hoped they hadn't heard him talking to Goo Fish Junior. Without a proper explanation, that might seem a bit strange, and he wanted to make a good first impression. He wasn't Zack, after all, who could walk into any room, tell a joke, and make friends.

But the students seemed too busy gawking at their new surroundings to have noticed. They weren't very talkative, either. They were probably tired and woozy from their own journeys. Making an effort, Billy smiled and nodded nervously at a few. He tried to think of something to say other than hello. But, smart as he was, he couldn't.

Finally, a thin redheaded boy, who seemed pretty

nervous himself, came closer and squinted at his name tag.

"So . . . Billy," he said. "I'm Ira. What's your project?"

Of course. It was a perfect question. They all had projects. Billy wished he'd thought of it but was just as happy to be asked.

"I'm using electroencephalography to image brain waves of . . . ," he began. Remembering the Power Rangers' befuddled reactions, he stopped himself. "I guess I should probably explain what *electroencephalography* means . . ."

A few of the students who were listening laughed nervously.

"Uh, did I say something wrong?" Billy asked.

Ira coughed a little and said, "No, not really. It's just that I think everyone here *knows* what *electroencephalography* means!"

A cheerful girl came up and pointed at the bowl in Billy's hands. "And does that adorable little *Carassius auratus* have a name?"

Knowing the Latin for goldfish, Billy brightened. "Goo Fish Junior," he said. Taking Ira's cue, he read her name tag. "What's your project, Alani?"

"I'm working on some spacecraft-navigation

software based on the shark's ability to sense the Earth's magnetic field," she said.

A black-haired teen with thick glasses raised his hand to speak, as if he were in a classroom. When they all turned his way, he said, "Hey, I'm Kevin and . . . uh, I know a joke. Why did the chicken cross the Möbius strip? To get to the same side!"

When they all laughed loudly, without anyone having to explain that a Möbius strip only *has* one side, it really broke the ice. Then they all started talking. In fact, Kevin reminded Billy a little of Zack.

Things kept getting better. During orientation, Billy learned that all the scientists working there, including the head of the center, the famous Dr. Anton Fent, would offer advice and guidance, but only if they were asked. He also found out that each student would have their own private lab space to use.

Billy was already feeling pretty great when he found his assigned space. One look at all the equipment made him give off a long, low whistle. "Wow!" he said. "With this, I can do in days what would've taken months, or a year, at Angel Grove High!"

Happily, he unpacked and made sure Goo Fish Junior's feeding schedule was up to date.

But then he heard a dreadful clatter from the hall outside his door. Relaxed as he was, Billy's Power Ranger instincts kicked in. When he opened the door and saw some suspicious shadows shifting in the hall, his first thought was that it was one of Rita Repulsa's monsters, thanks to the overall stench!

Rushing outside, Billy almost exhaled when he saw who was causing the racket.

Almost, but not quite.

It was Farkas "Bulk" Bulkmier and Eugene "Skull" Skullovitch, the two hapless bullies from back home. Dressed in gray overalls, Bulk and Skull were trying to pick up a bucket and mop they'd knocked over. Every time they tried, though, they somehow managed to keep bumping each other.

Billy loudly cleared his throat. "What are you two doing here?" he asked.

Startled, they both nearly fell over. Once they realized it was the "loser" they knew from Angel Grove High School, they straightened and did their best to look tough.

Bulk huffed. "So it's our old pal, Billy Cranston. You're one of the nerd types crawling all over this place, huh? It just so happens that Skull and I have decided to engage in some gainful employment here, as temporary custodial engineers."

Billy shook his head at the illogicality. "You two never cared about work before," he said. "And if you don't like 'nerd types,' why take a job that leaves you stuck with us for a week?"

Skull scrunched his face. "Hey," he said, "we're not stuck here with you. You're stuck here with us!"

Bulk patted his friend on the shoulder. "Exactly! When we heard there'd be as much free food as you can eat and a bunch of losers to push around, we signed right up with our fake IDs! And you'd better not get any ideas about turning us in, or else!"

Once, Billy might have let them push him around. Heck, fish used to scare him! But his experiences as a Power Ranger had given him confidence, even if he couldn't tell them about his other identity.

Billy wasn't used to standing up for himself, especially not to Bulk and Skull, but he held his ground. "Or else what, Bulk?" he asked.

Bulk grinned. "You know."

Billy felt unsure what to do next, but he crossed his arms over his chest. "No, Bulk, I don't," he said. "Why don't you tell me?"

Confused by Billy's confident stance, Bulk fumbled for the right words. "Or else . . . you know. It'll be trouble for you, not the other way around."

Pursing his lips, Skull echoed his partner's words. "Yeah, trouble."

With that, the two strutted off as if they owned the island—but not without nearly tripping again over the bucket and mops they carried.

Relieved his act had worked, Billy realized it could have been worse. *Bulk and Skull are a nuisance,* he thought. *But at least they're not a real threat.*

Chapter 4

As the Blue Ranger returned to his lab, he failed to notice a short alien figure skulking among the shadows farther down the hall. As the figure neared the open area that contained the big tanks, sunlight from the domed glass ceiling shone on his doglike features.

Afraid he might be seen, Finster stepped back into the shadows. The evil minion couldn't care less about all the busy teens and scientists. He was much more interested in the enormous marine specimens. But he was also in a hurry.

Using alchemical magic on the Moon Palace teleporter to get through the solar storm had been easy. Going to Earth without Rita's permission was dangerous, though. If the wicked queen awoke from her nap and found Finster gone before he could prove the value of his Enhancifier by creating his greatest monster ever, she'd be . . . well . . . *unhappy*, to say the least.

Once Finster made it to the collection of enormous tanks, seeing all the monstrous possibilities made him so giddy, his worries disappeared. As he "shopped" around, checking out one marine creature after another, it was all he could do to keep himself from clapping like a child in a toy store.

Now, now, he reminded himself. *I'm a scientist and an inventor. There'll be plenty of time for giddy clapping later. This is a time for clear thinking! My choice has to be perfect!*

The blue whale in the biggest tank caught his eye immediately. Pressing his hands against the thick Plexiglas for a closer look, Finster thought his mission might already be accomplished.

But something made him hesitate.

Is it really the best I can do? he wondered.

True, the whale was enormous. It was, of course, as big as a whale! But there was something too . . . *peaceful* about the giant. It made Finster worry whether it had the heart to attack anyone, let alone the Mighty Morphin Power Rangers.

"This is more like it!" he said, turning to the next tank. "The great white shark is a classic killing machine! Still . . . classic can also be cliché. I want something even more impressive."

Like a picky shopper, he found something wrong with nearly every choice. The giant spined sea star, with its ability to regrow limbs, or the giant spider crab, with its armor-like exoskeleton, were fearsome, but . . . not quite as big as Finster wanted.

The billowing, poisonous tentacles of the lion's mane jellyfish were much more like it!

Or the Portuguese man-of-war!

Or the giant isopod!

Strengthened by his Enhancifier, any one of them could crush the Power Rangers.

Soon he had the opposite problem. There were too *many* great choices.

This will be a tough decision, he thought, chuckling. *A tough decision, indeed!*

Chapter 5

Back in his student lab, a certain teen with attitude had filled Goo Fish Junior's little glass bowl with waterproof sensors, speakers, and microphones. Billy hoped they would not only record the fish's brain waves, but also let Billy "talk back" with sounds, lights, or bubbles, whichever worked best for a goldfish. Color-coded wires led from the bowl, across the worktable and floor to a high-powered computer. From there, they were connected to a fancy headset that Billy wore.

Ready for his first try, Billy leaned in close to the bowl. "Goo Fish Junior, hello!" he said. "Can you hear me?"

As he spoke, the tiny speakers sent waves through the water, a gentle light flashed Morse code, and a little tube gave off a sequence of bubbles.

When Goo Fish Junior seemed to bubble back, Billy got incredibly excited.

Did it work? he wondered. *What will the fish say?*

But the computer only translated: "Blorp, boop, blop."

"Oh well," Billy said to the fish. "At least I proved the equipment works. Once I make some changes to the sensors, I should be able to *see* what you're thinking. Maybe then the computer can create a better version of fish-speak. You probably only want to tell me how crowded it is in there, anyway, huh? This is going to take a little soldering . . ."

No sooner did Billy find the soldering iron than there was a knock at the door.

"Come—" he said.

Before he finished the invitation, a very hurried and very *wet* Ira and Alani charged in. They were followed by a group of other students. Together, they made Billy's lab almost as crowded as the fishbowl.

And it wasn't just Ira and Alani who were wet—everyone was. At first, Billy thought they'd gone swimming, but they seemed upset.

"What's wrong, guys?" he asked.

Ira bent over to shake some of the water from his hair, as he explained, "These two custodial engineers spilled their bucket on us! I'm not even sure they *meant* to do it. They were tripping all over the place, so it could have been an accident. But when I asked them to apologize, they called us losers and said they'd do it again!"

Alani was fuming. "Custodial engineers, ha!" she said. "I don't think they've had any janitorial training at all!"

Randal, a blond boy, looked especially shaken up. He leaned against the doorframe and sadly wrung his shirt dry. "I really hate this," he said. "It's bad enough that I have to deal with bullies back home. How am I going to complete a decent aquatic toxicology study if I'm constantly looking over my shoulder?"

Feeling bad for his new friends, Billy passed around the few towels he'd packed and sighed. "Unfortunately," he said, "I'm very familiar with those two. But trust me, you don't have to worry about them anywhere near as much as you do your own fear. If you stand up to Bulk and Skull, they'll back off. I promise."

Randal twisted his brow as tightly as he had his shirt. "No offense, Billy, but not worrying is easier said than done for some of us. I mean, look at you. You're so sure of yourself, it's hard to believe you were ever *really* afraid of something."

Me? Sure of myself? Billy thought. *I guess being a Power Ranger really has changed me for the better. But that doesn't help them much.*

"I *have* been very afraid," Billy said to Randal. "I've had huge fears, so bad I couldn't move! It started back in grade school. I was trying to create a self-sustaining whirlpool in a lake, but the vortex balance was just a little off."

"That can happen to anyone," Ira offered. "And you used your finger to correct it?"

"Exactly. And when I did," Billy continued, "I guess a fish must have mistaken my finger for a worm. Before I knew what was happening, for lack of a better word . . . *chomp*!"

Billy said it so loudly that everyone jumped a little.

He held up his finger and looked at it. "There's no scar, even a tiny mark, but I still remember that bite as if it happened yesterday. After that, for years, I couldn't bring myself to go in any water where there *might* be fish. I'd go to the beach sometimes, but I'd never swim. I'd even stay at least ten yards from the shoreline. I actually said no to scuba diving with my friends. But then . . ."

Billy paused. They all waited eagerly for him to

finish, but it occurred to him that he couldn't exactly tell them how his goldfish's namesake, the monstrous Goo Fish, had immobilized his fellow Power Rangers. The Blue Ranger was the last member of the team left standing. Billy couldn't let them down; he had to do something, no matter how hard it was.

Finally he said, "My friends needed me, so I had to face my fear and get over it. And now . . ." As everyone watched, without hesitating, he stuck his finger into the goldfish bowl. Goo Fish Junior nibbled at it, but the tiny mouth didn't even tickle. "I've conquered my fear."

His fellow "nerd types" were very impressed.

Ira looked downright inspired. "Billy's right! We should stand up to those bullies together, as a team!"

The others nodded. Billy was going to say something else, but Randal, still in the doorway, glanced outside and gulped.

"It's them!" he shouted. "They're coming this way! We've got to get out of here and hide!"

All at once, the frightened teens raced out.

"Wait!" Billy called. He headed after them, but by the time he reached the door, they'd disappeared down the hall. He saw a grinning Bulk and Skull coming from the other direction. They picked up their pace to chase the students.

But Billy stepped out to block their path. "Hey! I want to talk to you! Those guys are really afraid of you."

The two slowed down to face him. Pleased with himself, Bulk snickered. "Yeah, well, that's the point, isn't it?"

"No, it's not the point of anything," Billy said. Although Trini was able to translate for Billy sometimes, none of the Rangers understood how Bulk and Skull thought. "I want you to back off and leave them alone!" he said.

Billy was so loud and confident, it made them shake. Wondering why he was talking so tough, they peered over Billy's shoulder into the lab.

"Your martial arts pal Jason isn't around anywhere, is he?" Bulk asked.

Seeing that the lab was empty of people, they relaxed.

Noticing the fishbowl, though, Skull's eyes lit up. "Oh! Oh! A fishy!" he said.

As excited as a little boy on his birthday, Skull rushed in. Spotting the food container, he grabbed it and started shaking flakes into the bowl.

Billy turned toward Skull. "Stop that!"

Billy was about to take the food container from Skull, but a swaggering Bulk stepped into his path. Even as a civilian, Billy was sure he could move Bulk if he had to, but his Power Ranger training had taught him that violence was only to be used as a last resort. So even though it meant trying to explain something to Skull, Billy gave it his best shot.

"Overfeeding can hurt goldfish," he said. "They're opportunistic feeders. That means they eat as long as there's food and don't know how to stop."

Skull shook in a few more flakes. "Aw, overeating never bothered Bulk. I don't see why it'd hurt Little Bulky here."

"Little Bulky?" Bulk said, half smiling. "That's sweet. Wait. I don't overeat!"

"Please stop," Billy said.

Bulk sneered and aimed his thumb at the door. "Come on, Skull. We've got a whole island of losers to play with!"

When they left, Billy wanted to follow and find his friends. First, though, he had to scoop all the extra flakes out of the fishbowl. It was a long, difficult process, especially with the sensors getting in the way, but he was responsible for the fish's health.

As he worked, something about the way Goo Fish Junior tilted his body made Billy think he looked disappointed.

"Sorry," Billy said. "It's for your own good."

Once he was finished, Billy searched the halls. When he couldn't find Bulk and Skull, he hoped they'd decided to take a break from acting tough. He did find his fellow students, though. They were all together in the cafeteria.

Ira, Alani, and the others had pushed several tables together in the center of the space so everyone would fit. They were having what looked like a very serious meeting. A pile of chemical supplies had been stacked on the floor near their chairs.

Seeing Billy enter, Ira started a round of applause.

Billy half smiled, half frowned. "Thanks," he said, "but . . . what's going on? What's all that stuff?"

As he got closer, he realized that the students had gathered the standard chemical ingredients for stink bombs and flash firecrackers. They'd already made two large buckets of what looked like a powerful liquid glue.

An eager Alani bounced up from her seat. "We're

taking your advice!" she said proudly. "We're going to face our fear of those two bullies and get some payback!"

Billy shook his head. "Wait, no! That's *not* what I meant. If you try to get revenge, you're just stooping to their level."

"Oh no, not at all," Randal said. He pointed at the supplies. "What we've got planned is *much* more sophisticated than anything Bulk and Skull could come up with. Clearly, we are *way* above their level."

"That's not what I meant," Billy said. "You're just becoming bullies yourselves!"

Ira frowned. "But isn't that okay, if you only bully bullies?" he asked.

"No," Billy said. "It isn't."

"Why not?" Alani asked.

Trying to figure out how best to explain, Billy looked off to gather his thoughts. When he did, he saw something very strange in the distance, over by the marine specimen tanks. It was a short, furry figure, clapping happily. At first Billy thought it was Bulk or Skull, but as he narrowed his eyes, the pointy dog ears he saw were unmistakable.

It was Finster!

Without another thought, Billy ran from the cafeteria.

"Sorry!" he called back to the others. "I have to go check on something extremely important. We'll talk later, but please, don't make any more plans until we do!"

Once he was sure that the students couldn't see him, Billy pulled out his Power Morpher and yelled, "It's Morphin Time!"

Chapter 6

Each of the Morphers that Zordon had given the five Power Rangers contained an ancient Power Coin imbued with primal energy. The Power Morphers looked a little like oversize belt buckles, but could easily fit in their pockets. To activate his, Billy held it in his right fist with his left hand open. At the same time, he called out the name of the prehistoric beast from which his Power Coin drew its power:

"Triceratops!"

In a flash of crackling light, he morphed. Billy Cranston's strength, speed, and durability were greatly enhanced—and he now wore the helmeted uniform of the Blue Ranger!

Even though Finster was far off among the tanks, his eyes snapped toward the flash.

"I'd know that flash of light anywhere!" he said to himself. "It's one of *them*!" With a high-pitched, cowardly squeal, the short alien turned and ran.

Quickly as he could, he rushed behind one of the largest tanks, where he hoped he'd be out of sight.

If one of Rita's minions is here, Billy thought, *there aren't a lot of conclusions I can draw other than trouble.*

As the distance to the tanks disappeared beneath the Blue Ranger's racing feet, his instincts told him to contact the rest of his team.

"Power Rangers, emergency!" he said into his wrist-communicator.

He expected to hear Jason, or one of the others, but all Billy got in response was crackling static: *Kshhscrkl!*

Of course, he realized. *The solar flares are still interfering!*

The Blue Ranger was on his own.

"Finster isn't exactly a fighter," Billy mused. "At least if he's by himself, I might have a better chance of stopping him on my own."

Unfortunately, the Blue Ranger soon learned that Finster was *not* alone. As he reached the far side of the tank, Billy found himself staring at a small squadron of the faceless foot soldiers known as the Putty Patrol.

The pack of gray humanoids came at him, ready

for a fight. When the first reached him, he managed to grab it by the arm and flip it into another. But there were too many for him to continue fighting hand to hand. If Billy didn't do something soon, they could overwhelm him.

He un-holstered his blade blaster and fired. Laser-like flashes flew at the rushing Putty Patrollers. Two Putties were hit and knocked right off their feet, but that didn't stop the rest. Whether he could reach his teammates or not, Billy still needed extra help.

It was a good thing that, thanks to the coins, each Power Ranger also had a special weapon they could call on when needed.

"Power Lance!" he cried.

At the Blue Ranger's words, the double-headed lance, nearly as tall as Billy, magically appeared above him. It seemed to float for a moment. The blue-white sparks that surrounded it looked like a miniature lightning storm. Then it fell into his waiting hands, fitting Billy's grip like a comfortable pair of gloves.

The timing couldn't have been better. The first of the Putty Patrol was just about to reach him. Billy held the lance out with both hands and spun. He moved so hard and fast, the front row of Patrollers was knocked aside.

So far, so good, but how long can I keep this up? he wondered.

Billy was confident in his ability to use his mind, and he had proven his bravery to Zordon and his fellow Power Rangers a thousand times. On the other hand, he wasn't a martial artist, like black belt Jason or Trini. His limited combat style didn't come close to Zack's Hip Hop Kido, or the hard-hitting moves of gymnast Kimberly.

But he had them *all* as friends and teachers.

Besides, he thought, *Jason's always telling me that at least as much fighting is done with your head as it is with your fists.*

His current opponents, on the other hand, were not big thinkers. The Putty Patrol rushed at him any which way. They had no plan at all nor even a very good sense of what they should do when they reached the Blue Ranger, other than try to hit him.

They weren't even sure which should attack first.

It made sense. Billy knew well that Finster had created the Putty Patrollers to overcome enemies with their numbers rather than with strategy. He realized that if he could knock enough of them out of the fight, the rest would fall, like a house of cards.

As his confidence increased, he imagined Jason smiling and saying, "That's what I mean by using your head to fight!"

It was tough going, but the Blue Ranger worked at it. Rather than panic, he went step-by-step, taking his time to avoid making stupid mistakes. He twirled his lance, knocking out another two Patrollers, then butted some more with the tip, one at a time, before twirling again.

Remembering how Kimberly had advised him to use all his limbs, Billy leaned back and kicked one Patroller into another. As he came back to standing, he thrust the lance at a Patroller right in front of him, then pulled it back to hit another trying to take him from behind. Twirling the lance to his left with one hand, he scattered a group on one side, at the same time using his free fist to punch another on his right.

Finally, he split the Power Lance into two, trident-like Sai blades. Using the flats of the blades, he swatted the remaining Patrollers. Soon enough, they were all limping off. Scattered and battered, they collapsed back into the shapeless clay from which they were fashioned.

I did it! I got them all in less than two minutes! Billy thought. *But this is no time to congratulate myself. I have to find Finster.*

Pivoting this way and that, the Blue Ranger scanned every direction, but there was no sign of the wicked minion. The water in the tanks, lit by a huge skylight in the high ceiling, cast long, wavy shadows, creating lots of places to hide. Most likely, though, Rita's canine-like minion was back at the Moon Palace by now.

Even though Billy had beaten them, the Putty Patrol had served their purpose. They'd given Finster the time he needed to escape. At the same time, the Blue Ranger had a funny feeling that things weren't over yet, so he decided to keep searching, just in case.

Chapter 7

Finster couldn't leave, whether he wanted to or not. His mission was incomplete. So while the Blue Ranger battled the Putty Patrol, the stocky alien scrambled to a concealed spot along the building's far wall. There, scores of barrels filled with different types of food for the marine creatures were stacked high.

Some of the barrels were wrapped in protective tarps to keep the food in them cool and fresh. Desperate to keep out of sight, Finster grabbed one of the tarps and, despite an awful fishy smell, crouched beneath it and whimpered.

This is madness! Finster thought. *Normally, I would have teleported back to the Moon Palace the moment that Power Ranger saw me—but if I return to Rita without proof that my Enhancifier works, I'll have to explain why I left in the first place. She'll be furious!*

Peeking out from beneath the tarp, Finster watched nervously as the Blue Ranger kept searching.

When he came close, Finster ducked back under and held his breath. That part was easy enough, given the fishy smell.

At least it looks like there's only one Power Ranger here, he thought. *Better yet, from what Rita told me, the blue one is convinced he's not a good fighter. Not that I've ever fought anything myself. I did have to wrestle a loose steam tube on the Monster-Matic once, but that's about it. I'll have to think of ways to fight him without fighting him!*

He'd been holding his breath so long that when the Blue Ranger moved on, Finster gulped in some of the foul air and nearly gagged.

But first, he thought, *I need a new hiding place.*

With Billy gone, the bullied students in the cafeteria went back to making plans.

"We're not going to hurt them," Ira said. "We're just going to show Bulk and Skull that we won't be pushed around, right?"

They all nodded bravely, until Bulk and Skull swaggered in. The mere sight of them brought back their fear. Immediately, the students abandoned the comfortable tables they'd pushed together and scurried off to crowd around a small corner table, hoping to be left alone.

Seeing them, Bulk was tickled. Back home at Angel Grove High School, he'd never gotten a reaction this strong. Puffing up his chest and raising his voice, he said to them, "That's right! You all stay there until we're done with our lunch!"

When a few nodded nervously, he happily slapped Skull on the shoulder.

"See?" Bulk said. "They know who's in charge here!"

"Right!" Skull answered. But then he frowned. "Who?"

Bulk sighed. He liked Skull, but there were times when he didn't seem to get even the simplest rules about bullying. Using his thumb, Bulk pointed, first at himself, then at Skull.

"Us!" Bulk said. "*We're* in charge, of course!"

"Oh," Skull said. He nodded as if he understood but kept frowning.

They strutted along a row of heated serving trays, filling their plates with enough to feed a dozen people. All the while, Skull was still thinking about what Bulk had said.

Finally he asked, "Isn't Willy, the head janitor, in charge of us, Bulk?"

Bulk gritted his teeth. "Yes, but *aside* from him, we get to say what's what."

Reaching the long row of tables the "nerds" had left, Bulk and Skull plopped into two seats without looking. Just as Bulk was ready to dig in to his meal, he smelled something funny. He sniffed his food. It smelled fine; delicious, actually. He looked around and saw the students' stacked supplies on the floor near their chairs.

One of the buckets had spilled its contents, splashing bits of goo everywhere.

"Hey, losers!" Bulk said. "You were so scared of us, you knocked over your smelly science-nerd experiment when you ran off!"

The students gasped. Even if Bulk didn't know what was in that bucket, they did. But they didn't know how to explain it without angering him.

Ira, pushed to his feet by the others, cleared his throat and said, "Sorry. I really should clean that up before it sets. It's easy, all you need is—"

Bulk shook a warning finger at Ira, cutting him off. "Not now," he said. "You clean it up when we're done eating."

"No, you don't understand," Ira said. "That's—"

"Not another word!" Bulk said.

"Yeah!" Skull echoed. "We're in charge here!"

Ira shrugged and went back to his friends. Not sure what to do, the students whispered among themselves, occasionally pausing to glance nervously at Bulk and Skull.

Seeing them look at him, Skull smiled and waved.

Bulk elbowed him in the ribs. "Don't be nice to them! We're bullies, remember?"

But Bulk's elbow didn't just push Skull, it pushed his chair along with him. Bulk, not noticing, went back to eating. Skull was puzzled, though, so he looked down at his seat.

Some of the goo from the bucket had splashed on it.

Curious, Skull tried to shift himself closer to the table. When he did, the chair moved with him again.

"Hey, Bulk," he said. "Do your pants feel kind of strange?"

Bulk kept chewing as he answered. "Strange like what? Like my pants want to get up and dance?"

This time, Skull tried to stand, but he couldn't. "No," he said. "It's more like, even if you did want to get up and dance, your pants wouldn't let you."

Bulk stopped eating to stare at his friend. When Bulk tried to shift in his seat, his chair moved with him, too. Not only their butts, but their legs were stuck!

The "losers" watching from across the cafeteria tittered nervously.

"Uh . . . sorry?" Ira said.

When Bulk angrily rose, taking the chair along with him, they all ran out.

Still worried that Finster hadn't left, the Blue Ranger kept looking for him. As the afternoon wore on, the wavy shadows in the huge space near the tanks grew even deeper and longer. With all the dark areas, Billy might never be absolutely sure the evildoer had gone, but his instincts told him to keep trying.

He was making a third pass around the tanks when he heard some loud shouts and running feet coming from the halls behind him.

It could be another attack! he thought.

He sprinted toward the noise. It was coming from the long, wide corridor that led to the cafeteria. Reaching it, he stopped short, just out of sight of at least a dozen running, terrified students.

"Hurry!" Ira screamed. "They're gaining on us!"

"But we tried to warn them about the glue!" Alani said.

"I don't think they care!" Randal shouted.

Not knowing who or what they were fleeing, the Blue Ranger stayed hidden. *If it's another Putty Patrol,* he thought, *I can wait until they pass, then leap out behind them and take them by surprise!*

As the frightened students passed without seeing the Power Ranger, Alani pointed to a sign on the shiny floor ahead of them.

It said CAUTION—WET FLOOR WAX.

"Watch out for the floor!" she warned the others. Understanding, the students slowed down until they reached a turn, then sped along safely.

The hidden Blue Ranger, meanwhile, had been expecting to surprise some monsters. As it turned out, he was the one who was surprised, as a growling Bulk and Skull came hobbling down the hall. Seeing them wasn't the surprise so much as the strange way they were running: bent over and waddling—stuck to chairs!

It was all the Blue Ranger could do to keep from laughing. But when they ignored the sign and hit the waxed floor, Bulk fell sideways and Skull went sailing over him. Billy winced. He sort of felt bad for them, even if they were always asking for trouble.

Looking angry and dazed, they got back up

and went back to the chase, chairs and all. As they turned the same corner as the fleeing students, Billy wondered if he should step in to protect them.

I'd probably only have to show my face to break things up, he thought. *But then I'd have to explain why a Power Ranger is at the research center. If Finster's gone, I don't want to worry everyone for nothing.*

But then Ira's loud voice carried down the hall. "This is ridiculous!" he said. "There are only two of you, and we're sick of running!"

The sound of rushing footsteps continued, but now it was different. Instead of getting softer and farther away, it got louder and closer.

When Bulk and Skull came back around the corner, *they* were the ones with the frightened, panicked faces. The students came up behind them, looking determined and gaining ground.

"Bulk!" Skull screamed. "They turned the tables! Or is it the chairs?!"

"Never mind!" Bulk said. "I've got an idea. On three, do exactly what I do. One . . . two . . . sit!"

As the bullies reached the waxed part of the floor, they put the bottoms of their chair legs down. Rather than fall, they slid along in their chairs, gaining some distance on the students. They got back up to run without skipping a beat.

"That was fun!" Skull said.

"Not if they catch us, it won't be!" Bulk said.

Billy was pleased. Maybe his new friends had gone overboard with the glue, but Bulk and Skull could take care of themselves. And the Blue Ranger had bigger concerns. Even if Finster was gone, he'd been there for a reason. And how had he gotten past the solar flares to teleport?

He tried his wrist-communicator again.

"Rangers? Alpha 5?" he said.

But all he got in response was static.

Chapter 10

Huffing and puffing, Bulk and Skull headed for one of the few safe places they knew at the research center—Billy Cranston's laboratory space. With the Blue Ranger still searching for Finster, it was empty.

Inside, Bulk crouched at the entrance, nervously looking up and down the hall before closing the door.

"I think . . . I think we lost them," he said.

"Phew!" Skull said. He plopped onto the chair still glued to his pants. "Huh. You know, it's kind of handy being stuck to a chair. At least now I don't have to go looking for one when I want to sit down."

Bulk made a face but didn't bother answering. "See if you can find a pair of scissors or something," he said. "Maybe we can cut ourselves free."

As Bulk looked through the lab's cabinets and drawers, Skull's eyes went straight to the goldfish bowl. Ignoring Billy's warning, he smiled, slid over, and tapped in some more flakes from the food bottle.

While the fish ate, Skull put the backs of his hands to his own cheeks and made a fish face at it. When Goo Fish Junior happened to turn his way to get at some more of the food, Skull's face brightened.

"Hey! I think Little Bulky likes me!" Skull said.

Bulk looked up from his search and rolled his eyes. "Will you leave that fish alone?" But then his head snapped toward the hallway. "Quiet! I think I heard something!"

Worried, he waddled over and put his ear flat against the closed door.

Skull stared at him. "We're not really afraid of a bunch of losers, are we?" he asked.

"Of course not!" Bulk said. "We're only afraid of what we'd do to them if they caught us!"

But then his eyes went wide as saucers. "Ah! I think it's them! They're right outside! Quick! Hide! Hide!"

The two rushed about looking for a safe spot.

"Where? Where?" Skull cried.

When they got too close to each other, the metal legs of their chairs tangled. Now they weren't only stuck to the seats, they were stuck to each other! Spinning in a circle, they grabbed at the air as if they could hold on to it and pull themselves free.

Once their twisting and turning untangled the chair legs, they stumbled toward opposite ends of the room. Still trying to find a hiding spot, Bulk looked under the tables while Skull looked inside the desk drawers.

Seeing a tall supply cabinet, Bulk pulled it open. It was full of scientific equipment. Not knowing or caring what it was, he started yanking the equipment out and tossing it onto the floor.

Once it was empty, Bulk frantically waved at Skull.

"In here! Hurry up!" he said.

At first it seemed as if they'd never both make it inside. The cabinet was a tight fit, and the chairs made it harder. It was only when Skull, his chair and all, sat on Bulk's lap that they succeeded. Reaching out with all four hands, they forced the door shut.

"I can't see, anyway, so I'm closing my eyes," Skull said.

"Fine," Bulk answered. "Just stay quiet!" Then he closed his eyes, too.

Not used to being chased by "science nerds," their hearts beat so loudly, they didn't even hear the laboratory door swing open.

And they definitely didn't see Finster rush inside.

"Oh dear, oh dear," Finster muttered to himself. "All those teen scientists running around out there must be trying to find me! But how do they even know I'm here? And why are they so angry? They're probably working with that dratted Blue Ranger! I suppose it doesn't matter. The important thing is to hide somewhere until they give up."

Being something of a scientist himself, Finster quickly realized that the only place in Billy's lab that was large enough to hide inside was the supply cabinet.

Pleased with his brilliance, he chuckled as he grabbed the handle. *Given my height, this should be quite a comfortable place to wait them out!* he thought.

As the cabinet door opened, Bulk and Skull expected to see a group of angry science nerds. When they saw a furry, pointy-eared alien instead, they were very surprised.

Finster was also startled. He wasn't sure what he was staring at.

It looks sort of human, but it has two heads! he thought. *Is it some sort of monster the scientists here created? It's fascinating!*

As Bulk and Skull fell forward, a curious Finster

stepped back to give them room. The combined weight of the bullies broke the chairs, freeing them.

Still on the floor, they looked up at Finster and screamed. *"Ahhhh!"*

Finster, thinking they might be trying to form their own low-tech version of a Megazord, screamed back. *"Ahhhh!"*

Bulk and Skull scrambled to their feet and ran toward the door.

Skull's voice became very squeaky. "Bulk, wha-what is it?"

Nearly out the door, a terrified Bulk said, "I don't know. Maybe it's some kind of revenge experiment those crazy science nerds sent after us! Keep running!"

Peh. They're just a pair of frightened human teens, Finster realized. *And I have my own problems. Should I head back to the Moon Palace and face Rita's wrath or wait until the excitement dies down, sneak back to the tanks, and use one of those wonderful giant creatures to create my ultimate monster?*

Imagining the fearsome creature he might create, Finster closed the laboratory door and took the human teens' hiding place in the cabinet.

Running full tilt through the hallways, Bulk and

Skull began screaming at the top of their lungs, “Out of the way! We’ll get you for this!”

They were so loud, the Blue Ranger couldn’t help but hear them. The sound also made it easy for him to find them. But he had to yank them by their collars just to slow them down. The hardest part was to get them to stop yelling long enough to explain what they were screaming about.

“Guys, it’s okay,” he said over their cries.

When they finally recognized that a Power Ranger had grabbed them, they stopped struggling.

“Easy for you to say! You didn’t see that monster!” Skull said.

“Whatever it is, it’s gone now,” the Blue Ranger said. “What sort of monster did you see?”

Bulk panted. “It looked . . . sort of like . . . a really big Scottish terrier!” he said.

Skull leaned against the wall, breathless. “But it walked . . . on two legs,” he said, “and had a really horrible scream!”

“Finster,” the Blue Ranger said. “And where was this?”

Bulk pointed, but he was too out of breath to speak.

"Lab . . . ," Skull added. "The one . . . where that loser . . . Billy . . . works."

Loser? Billy thought. He stared at Skull for a moment, then decided to let it go.

As soon as they caught their breath, Bulk and Skull went back to running, even if they no longer had any idea where to go that would be safe from monsters and science nerds.

Chapter 11

The Blue Ranger paused at the door to his laboratory, his hand on the knob. He still had no idea why Finster was there, but now figured that the solar flares may have left him stranded, giving Billy only a few hours to catch him.

If he was trying to destroy the center by overrunning it with Putties, or unleashing one of his monsters, he'd have done it by now, Billy thought. *Besides, Rita Repulsa and her equally evil minions usually attack places like power plants, military bases, or big cities. Why a science lab?*

The only other possibility Billy could think of was that Finster was there looking for something, but what? There wasn't anything on the small, isolated island other than marine life.

Well, Billy thought, *it's time to find out!*

He quietly turned the knob. Then he threw open the door and leaped inside. The Blue Ranger landed in a combat stance: his legs spread for solid balance and his hands out, ready to strike.

But there was no one there. No one he could see, anyway.

I should have known Finster wouldn't just be sitting out in the open, he thought. *But trying to surprise him was worth a shot.*

Noticing the extra food flakes floating in Goo Fish Junior's bowl, Billy gritted his teeth. Annoying as it was, that was more than likely Skull's work. *At least that confirms this was where they saw Finster,* he thought. He'd have to clean out the bowl, *again,* later.

As he scanned the room, he kept up his guard. Unlike the large area that held the marine tanks, there weren't all that many places to hide in the lab. If Finster was still there, he'd be easy to find. The space was a mess. The equipment belonging to the research center, as well as Billy's things, had been broken, torn, and scattered everywhere. But none of the piles were tall enough to conceal even a short alien.

The largest pile was a heap of equipment on the floor near the supply cabinet. The strange collection, of circuit boards and what looked like parts of a microscope, was half covered by the pieces of a broken mirror. Unless Billy was mistaken, all of that used to be *in* the supply cabinet.

That's certainly a clue, Billy thought.

Hand on his holstered blaster, the Blue Ranger approached the cabinet. When he tugged at the handle, it resisted. Something inside was trying to keep the door closed.

Bingo! Billy thought.

With his enhanced strength, all he had to do was yank a little harder. The door flew open—and there was Finster. When Billy aimed the blaster at him, the cowardly minion shivered and raised his hands to cover his doglike face.

"Now, now! No shooting or hitting, please!" he begged. "I'm no warrior! More a thinker, you know. All that punching and kicking strikes me as crass."

It was true, Billy had never seen Finster in a fight. Then again, he hadn't often seen him without a monster nearby, either. To make sure they were alone, Billy looked around to see if anything was moving, but nothing was, and there were no other hiding spots.

Still cautious, he eyed Finster. "There's no need to fight if you just surrender," he said.

Lowering his hands, Finster chuckled. "Surrender?

That's a fine, fine joke! I really must tell the queen that one, once I get back and see her again. Ten thousand years in a space Dumpster, and you think I'd just *surrender*?"

For someone who wasn't a fighter, Finster seemed strangely confident.

Billy held the blaster steady. "You're not going anywhere," he said.

"I'm afraid I must disagree with you about that, Power Ranger," Finster answered. Straightening the tool smock he always wore, he waddled defiantly out of the cabinet.

"Electricus," Finster said. "Here's your target. Fry him."

"Electricus?" Billy said.

The room still looked empty. The Blue Ranger had no idea whom, or what, Finster was talking to. But then the pile of broken equipment started to move. It shifted around, assembling itself like a living puzzle. Soon it looked less and less like a heap of junk and more like a hastily made robot!

A satisfied Finster watched. "I *do* find violence crass," he said. "Unless it's one of my monsters being violent! Then it can be quite wonderful!"

Even when Electricus was finished putting itself together, it didn't have much of a shape, but a set of lenses on what might be considered its forehead flared to life, and . . .

A bright crimson beam shot across the room!

Billy leaped back to avoid being hit, then fired back with his blaster. He hit Electricus dead-on, but one of the broken pieces of mirror covering its body reflected the blast. It hit the wall, making a small, smoking hole.

Unharmed, Electricus made a high-pitched whining sound, then fired again.

Billy leaped a second time. Despite everything, he found himself impressed by the monster's design.

He looked at Finster and said, "That whine must be a feedback coil and a transistor boosting the voltage to recharge the laser. You could have gotten them from the lab equipment, and the capacitors you'd need from the circuit boards. The lenses are obviously from a microscope. But where did you get a laser head?"

Finster tried to get closer to the door, but the Blue Ranger blocked his way. Proud of his work, and seeing no reason not to answer a simple question, he said, "A laser pointer. Same principle. The hard part was adjusting the microscope lenses."

"Smart," Billy said. "But I've got a few ideas of my own!"

As Electricus charged its laser again, the Blue Ranger dove, rolled, and leaped up near the ceiling. There he tore some frosted glass covers off the lab's recessed lighting. When the next blast came his way, rather than dodge, he held the glass covers up as a shield. The ray hit the covers. The light that came out of the other side was bright but harmless.

It was Finster's turn to be impressed. "That's diffusing glass!" he said. "Clever! Laser is organized light, so you found a way to make it disorganized again!"

"Thanks. Want to tell me how you teleported here through the solar flares?" Billy asked.

"Ah," Finster said, "that means you don't know how! Which also means it's unlikely your fellow Power Rangers will be joining us any time soon. Excellent!"

Billy groaned at his mistake. Finster was very smart.

The minion's way to the door was clear. Again he headed for it.

"Much as I'd love to talk shop, Power Ranger, I really must be on my way," he said.

"I'm going to have to insist that you stay!" Billy said. He raced up and grabbed Finster around the waist. The moment his hands made contact with the inventor's tool smock, a painful electric pulse raced through the Blue Ranger.

"Yeow!" Billy cried out.

Rattled from head to toe, the Blue Ranger was forced to let go.

"Shocking, isn't it?" Finster laughed. "Oh, that's another one I must tell Rita! Shocking! Ha-ha! Goodbye!"

By fighting with his brain, Finster was giving Billy a lot more trouble than he'd expected. Billy promised himself he wouldn't underestimate Finster again.

"Okay, you electrified your smock," the Blue Ranger said. "But what happens if I do this?"

Rather than touch Finster's smock again, he grabbed him by the arms. Before the little alien realized what was happening, Billy lifted him off his feet and hurled him into Electricus. When the electrified tool smock made contact with Electricus, both were covered in bolts of jagged white light.

Electricus broke into pieces. Now it really was a pile of trash.

Smoke curling from his smock, a dazed Finster plopped down beside it. After grabbing the side of his head to steady himself, Finster sadly patted his invention.

"Poor thing," he said. "If I'd built you in my workshop, you could have really been something. Now I only have one choice left. I wish it hadn't come to this."

With a sigh, Finster took a small rectangular box from one of the smock's pockets. To Billy, it looked like a TV remote.

"On the bright side," Finster said, "I *did* make my Enhancifier back home!"

Before the Blue Ranger could react, Finster aimed the Enhancifier at the only other living thing in the room—the goldfish in the bowl. He pressed a button.

"I didn't intend this for such a small animal," Finster said, "but . . . you've left me no choice."

A sparkling ball of blue plasma shot from the Enhancifier into the bowl. Surrounded by the strange energy, Goo Fish Junior started to swell. At first he looked like a sponge, sucking in not only the weird energy, but everything else in the bowl, including the water, extra food, and Billy's inter-species communication experiment!

For a moment, as Goo Fish Junior completely filled the bowl, he became sphere-shaped. Then the glass shattered. As the shards flew across the lab, Billy had to shield his eyes. When he looked again, his goldfish was six feet tall!

He still had his tail and fish eyes and body, but he also had stubby arms and legs. There was a slimy coating all over the fish's body. Billy guessed it probably helped keep the gills moist so that Goo Fish Junior could breathe in the air.

Finster had turned him into one of his unnatural monsters!

"Goo Fish Junior!" Billy cried. "No!"

Chapter 12

The human-size Goo Fish Junior lurched around. Bumping into walls, tables, and equipment, he nearly fell off his new feet. The big goldfish seemed terribly confused by the sudden change.

Not wanting to hurt him, the Blue Ranger lowered his blaster.

Finster stood by a table. He was clearly thrilled to be watching his creation in action, but from the way Finster ducked whenever Goo Fish Junior stumbled too close, it didn't seem as if Finster could command him.

If he can't control Goo Fish Junior, that much is good news, Billy thought. *Maybe I can get him into one of the big tanks to keep him out of trouble. From there, I can try to figure out how to change him back.*

Billy put his arms out and tried to gently corral his former pet.

"Easy, fella," he said in his most soothing voice.

"Let's try to get you out into the hallway where there are fewer things to bump into, okay?"

It shouldn't be too hard, the Blue Ranger thought. *After all, how strong can a big goldfish be?*

As it turned out, a big goldfish could be very strong.

When Billy took another step closer, Goo Fish Junior spun on his feet and smacked him hard with his tail. The astonishing force of the blow took the Blue Ranger right off his feet and sent him sailing across the laboratory. His back hit the wall so hard that the plaster cracked.

He fell to the ground, landing with a loud thud.

The Blue Ranger's head was ringing, but he could still hear Finster applaud.

"Wonderful!" the giddy minion said. "Amazing, if I do say so myself!"

The door no longer blocked, Billy worried the evil inventor would escape. He fired his blaster at him, but missed. The blast burned a hole in the wall, making Finster howl.

All the racket made Goo Fish Junior even more frightened. The creature threw his short arms up in the air, puffed open his mouth, and gave off what could only be described as a fishy scream:

"Ahiehhhhhshh!"

Realizing that the frightening explosion was because of Billy's blaster, Goo Fish Junior stormed toward him and swatted him with his tail again. This time, the Blue Ranger flew straight up into the ceiling. His body went flat against the ceiling tiles. He seemed stuck there for a second, until some of the tiles, and the Blue Ranger, fell.

Finster was delighted. "That's it, my creation!" he shouted. "Destroy the Power Ranger!"

But instead, the big fish turned toward the loud, irritating noise that Finster was making.

"Not me!" Finster squealed. He pointed at the dazed Power Ranger and made the mistake of screaming even louder, "Him! Him!"

The noise only annoyed Goo Fish Junior more, so he kept coming.

At about the same time, both the Blue Ranger and Finster realized what the problem was. Finster said it first, though:

"You don't understand what I'm saying, do you?" Finster scratched his head. "Hmm. I really should have thought of that. All the monsters from the

Monster-Matic understand me completely. I can't very well go back to Rita unless I'm sure you know to attack the Blue Ranger, can I?"

With Goo Fish Junior nearly on him, Finster lowered his voice. "Sorry if I was shouting . . . but . . . Oh my. You don't understand *that,* either, do you?"

With a *THWACK* of the large golden tail, Finster went flying.

Since he was smaller than Billy, and not wearing a protective Power Ranger uniform, the tail knocked Finster out even before he landed in the supply cabinet. The force of the impact made the door slam shut, sealing him inside.

Billy got back on his feet. He was a little shaken, but he wasn't giving up. Much as he didn't want to hurt Goo Fish Junior, he also had to make sure he didn't hurt anyone else. And the research center was full of people.

He was about to summon the Power Lance again, thinking he could use it to force the confused creature toward the tanks, when he noticed something unusual on Goo Fish Junior's slimy, gold-scaled body. There were two big wires sticking out near his mouth—the wires from Billy's experiment!

Finster's weapon enlarged my communication equipment and made it part of that monstrous body, Billy thought. *But the wires are disconnected. If I can get close enough to reconnect them, maybe it'll be easier for us to communicate.*

The Blue Ranger's chance came sooner than he expected. In no time, Goo Fish Junior's mighty tail was flashing toward him again. This time, Billy saw it coming soon enough to leap up before it could hit him. Somersaulting in midair, he landed on the creature's back.

If Goo Fish Junior was scared before, having someone clinging to his back terrified him. He tried to pull Billy off, but neither his flashing tail nor his stubby arms could reach far enough to get him. Still, he bucked and twisted like a mechanical bull. All the while, the Blue Ranger tried to reach the wires near his mouth and reconnect them.

The gooey stuff on Goo Fish Junior's body also made it much harder to hang on. Billy had to use both arms and legs just to keep from falling off. Whenever he let go to reach for the wires, even with one hand, he started to slip off.

While the fearful Goo Fish Junior kept trying to

throw him, Billy squirmed closer to the wires. At last, he held both of the wires in the fingers of one hand. But all the movement made him start to slide away! At the last second, right before he tumbled to the floor, he managed to twist the wires together.

The wires gave off a little spark and a puff of smoke, but that didn't seem to hurt the big fish. He still looked more confused than anything else.

Now the question remained—had it worked? There was only one way to find out.

"Goo Fish Junior," Billy said.

The creature turned to the Blue Ranger. *But is it because of the noise, or because he recognized his name?* Billy thought. *He's not attacking, so that's a good sign.*

Billy said the fish's name again. "Goo Fish Junior, can you understand me?"

Being fish-shaped, the creature's neck couldn't nod up and down, but he bobbed his whole body, as if he understood.

Billy's experiment was a success!

But, changed by the alien technology, it did more than let Goo Fish Junior understand simple words. It also let the large goldfish talk back.

And the first thing he said to his owner was, "Feed me!"

Billy was a little taken aback. "Yes, Goo Fish Junior," he said. "I am the one who has been feeding you. Do you recognize me?"

"Yes," the big fish answered.

Thank goodness we're alone, otherwise someone might figure out my identity! Billy thought.

Goo Fish Junior wobbled and sounded sad. "Why do you not feed me more?" he asked.

"Because it's bad for you," Billy said. Talking this way made him feel strange, like he was a parent trying to tell a child not to have too much candy.

Goo Fish Junior kept wobbling. Now that he understood what Billy was saying, he didn't like what he was hearing.

"Bad?" he said. "But I'm always hungry! How can what my body wants be bad for me?"

Billy wasn't sure how to explain it in an easy way, but he tried. "Well," he said, "your body is made so it can live in lakes and ponds, and there isn't always food around. So to make sure you eat when there is food, it tells you to eat whenever you can. But here, there's so much food, it can make you sick!"

The fish's wobbling slowed. After a moment, it bobbed up and down again. "I think I understand," he said. "Then that means you have been taking care of me?"

Great, Billy thought. *Now we're getting somewhere. Maybe I can just ask him to get in one of the tanks.*

He smiled at Goo Fish Junior. "Yes, that's true! I've been taking care of you. I want you to be healthy."

At that moment, the door of the supply cabinet swung open. A groggy Finster stepped out. When he saw the giant goldfish and the Power Ranger standing side by side, he stopped short.

"Wait," he said. "What's going on here? Why isn't my monster destroying you?"

Goo Fish Junior wobbled. "Who is that? Why does he want me to hurt you?"

Rather than explain the entire history of Zordon, Rita Repulsa, and the Mighty Morphin Power Rangers, Billy said simply, "He wants to hurt me because he's the bad guy."

"You took care of me. Now I'll take care of you," Goo Fish Junior said. "By hurting the bad guy!"

"No!" the Blue Ranger said. "I don't want to hurt him; I just want him captured!"

But it was too late. The creature turned its tail toward Finster.

Finster's eyes went wide. "Wait," he said. "I'm the bad guy? Oh, that's right. I am!"

The tail swished. To avoid it, Finster hit the ground. The lower tip of the big fin barely touched his back.

"In that case," the alien inventor said, "I'd better get out of here!"

Low on the ground, Finster crawled between Goo Fish Junior's short legs, stood up, and bolted into the hallway. Billy chased after him, but this time, Finster didn't waste any time trying to hide.

He activated his teleporter.

Just before he vanished, Finster said to himself, "I only hope Rita is still napping!"

Chapter 13

With a dazzling flash of magic, Finster reappeared back at the Moon Palace, smack dab in the middle of his workshop. While he was at the Marine Island Research Center, he'd heard a constant bubbling sound, as the water in the big tanks was filtered to keep it clean. The halls of the Moon Palace were filled with a much more dreadful noise. It sounded like a foul wind pushing its way through a dark, desolate cave.

Realizing what it was, Finster relaxed.

"Rita's snoring," he said. "That means she's still asleep! Thank goodness! Now I can still go back to the research center and use my Enhancifier on an even bigger sea creature—and she'll be none the wiser. First, I need a way to get past that dratted Blue Ranger and his new fishy friend."

He puttered around, adjusting the dials on his faithful Monster-Matic this way and that. As he worked, he remembered how easily the Blue Ranger had figured out how Finster had assembled Electricus.

"A pity that particular Ranger must be destroyed," he thought. "He was one of the few beings I've met who actually seems to appreciate all the effort that goes into my work. Ah, well."

Knowing that the evil queen could wake up at any time, Finster stopped his adjustments. This was not the time to improvise; it was a time for action. Quickly, he filled the Monster-Matic with his special clay. Next he inserted the big steam-pressured molds that he used to mass-produce his simplest, but most handy monsters, the Putty Patrollers.

Once everything was in place, he fired up the machine. It hissed and groaned loudly.

Loud enough to wake the queen!

"Destroy! Crush! *Mrrbgglll!*" she said.

The sound of Rita Repulsa's voice, coming from all the way on the other side of the Moon Palace, nearly made Finster faint.

"Sh!" he said, slapping the Monster-Matic. It shouldn't have worked, but it did. The machine quieted down.

Rita, who'd apparently been talking in her sleep, went back to her snoring.

The machine was humming along now. In a few moments, it began pumping out fully cooked Putty Patrollers. One at a time, the monster foot soldiers were ejected from the exit tube at the Monster-Matic's far end.

Finster usually cheered whenever he produced a new monster, but under the circumstances, he had to stay silent. Every now and then, he heard Rita cackling, as if she'd dreamed something funny.

Rather than risk waking her by making too many monsters, Finster turned off the Monster-Matic. Then he activated his teleporter, taking his new Putty Patrol, and the Enhancifier, back to the research center.

Chapter 14

Meanwhile, back on Earth, the Blue Ranger had coaxed the man-size Goo Fish Junior out into the hall and was trying to get him to move toward the tanks.

"I can't put you in just *any* tank, Goo Fish Junior," Billy explained. "Goldfish need freshwater to be healthy, and a lot of the tanks here have salt water, like in the ocean. You can't breathe salt water."

He wasn't sure the creature understood completely, but Goo Fish Junior nodded in that funny way, bobbing his body up and down.

Having checked the research center logs on the computer in his now-messy lab, Billy discovered one tank that would be perfect. A twenty-foot-long freshwater beluga sturgeon had been released from it just yesterday, leaving it uninhabited. Empty now, except for the water, it would be perfect for a big goldfish. Unfortunately, that tank was also the farthest away, and getting Goo Fish Junior to move, even slowly, wasn't an easy task.

Strong as the monster-fish was, he wasn't used to being out in the open air, making him very skittish. Billy did his best to keep him calm. But there was only so much he could do.

Suddenly, loud screams came from down the hall: *Ahhhh!*

A quick glance told the Blue Ranger it was only Bulk and Skull. They were still being chased by the students. But the noise made Goo Fish Junior panic and run in the opposite direction.

"No, wait!" Billy said.

He headed after Goo Fish Junior to calm him down. Trying his best to be soothing, Billy patted the nervous creature on his slimy head. Seeing how afraid the creature was made Billy think about his old fears and realize how far he'd come.

At least this time I'm not afraid of fish, he thought.

Feeling sympathetic, he tried to imagine what all this was like for Goo Fish Junior.

"I guess things don't sound that loud when you're underwater, huh?" Billy said.

Goo Fish Junior quivered sadly. "No, they do *not*!" he answered.

Billy pointed at the distant, water-filled tanks. "That's why I want to get you back underwater, over there, so you'll be safe and sound."

At the same time, he was thinking, *And so that people will be safe from that tail of yours!*

At this rate, it would take hours to get Goo Fish Junior there, and that was time Billy could use to figure out how to change him back.

"I've got an idea, big guy," he said.

Billy knew that goldfish ears were inside their bodies, rather than outside, but they worked much the same way as any ear. He walked to Goo Fish Junior's side and, using his hands, covered the spots along his head where his inner ears were.

"How about if I do this while we walk?" Billy asked. "Is that better?"

Goo Fish Junior bobbed up and down. "Yes, it is! Stay there!"

Billy grinned. "Okay," he said. "But you have to promise not to hit me with your tail."

"Promise?" the fish answered. After a few steps, he asked, "What's promise?"

Before Billy could explain, there was a big flash of blinding light. Finster and his new Putty Patrol teleported in just a few yards in front of them!

Exasperated, the evil minion shook his head and said, "Did you have to be standing *right* here?"

"It's the bad guy!" the goldfish howled.

Frightened again, Goo Fish Junior spun, accidentally swatting the Blue Ranger.

"Uhn!" Billy said as he hit the wall.

Finster waved the Putty Patrol forward. "Destroy them!" he commanded. "And if you can't manage that, at least *delay* them!"

Billy was back on his feet and ready for action in less than a second. He expected Goo Fish Junior to run, but he didn't. He was fighting back!

The Blue Ranger was tired of being smacked by that big fish tail. At the same time, he enjoyed seeing it swat the Putty Patrollers. As Goo Fish Junior swung his tail, the Putties flew into the air two at a time. But there were too many for a frightened goldfish to handle, even if he was pretty big. Goo Fish Junior needed help, and who better to help than a Power Ranger?

"Power Lance!" Billy cried.

In an instant, it was in his hands.

As Billy twirled the Power Lance and Goo Fish Junior swung his tail, they made a steady path through the middle of the Putty Patrol.

As the battle continued, a running Bulk and Skull briefly appeared down the hall. Once they saw what was going on, they shrieked and skidded to a stop, nearly hitting each other.

Then they ran back the way they had come.

Focused on the fight, Billy was pleased he and Goo Fish Junior were winning, but he also remembered the last fight. Finster had used the Putty Patrol as a distraction to get away.

As he battled, he kept his eye on the inventor. This time, Rita's evil henchman didn't run away to hide. Instead, he made his way far down among the tanks. The Blue Ranger knew what Finster was up to: He was planning to make another monster! But there wasn't much Billy could do about it, as long as he was surrounded by Putty Patrollers. He couldn't very well leave Goo Fish Junior to fight on his own.

Before he could figure out what to do, the students who had been chasing Bulk and Skull stopped at the entrance of the room. Unlike the bullies, when they saw the fight, they didn't run.

"It's the Blue Power Ranger, and he needs help!" Ira said.

"But what can we do?" Alani asked.

"Well," Randal said. "We're still carrying all the tricks we were going to use on Bulk and Skull before Billy talked us out of it. How about we use those on these monsters?"

Everyone nodded in agreement. Before the Blue Ranger could stop them, the brave students entered the fray. Soon the air was filled with the terrific stench of stink bombs and the bright, confusing light of flash firecrackers. Randal took the biggest chance, by sneaking up closer and pouring some slippery oil on the floor right at the foot soldiers' feet.

The Putty Patrollers slipped and slid into Goo Fish Junior's waiting tail. Swat after swat, they were sent into a pool of the sticky goo that had stuck Bulk and Skull to their chairs.

The tide of the battle was clearly turning. The Blue Ranger was still worried about the students, but seeing how they handled themselves, he also saw his chance to stop Finster.

If Finster makes another monster with that new weapon, things will get a lot more dangerous for everyone! he thought. So he started moving.

But when Goo Fish Junior saw Billy leaving, he

followed the Blue Ranger out.

"Cover my ears! Cover my ears!" he called out.

"In a minute, Goo Fish Junior! Right now I have to stop that bad guy!" Billy said.

Ahead, Finster was standing right next to the tank that held the Portuguese man-of-war.

"Imagine what will happen once I use the Enhancifier on you!" Finster said as he aimed his device.

Billy did imagine just that. With a shape like a giant jellyfish and tentacles over fifty meters long that could deliver a fatal sting, the creature was already as dangerous and frightening as most monsters. Goo Fish Junior was trouble enough, but a huge Portuguese man-of-war would be a disaster.

I have to do something, and fast! he thought.

Keeping his Power Lance in one hand, the Blue Ranger drew his blaster. The two weapons could be combined into one, but rather than take the time, he fired a single shot from the blaster and hit the Enhancifier.

A startled Finster leaped as the box in his hands glowed hot and shattered. When he realized what had happened, the furious inventor licked a burnt finger and stamped his feet.

"Oh . . . drat!" he said. He turned to the Blue Ranger. "Now look what you've done!"

Not taking any chances, Billy raced up and lowered the tip of the Power Lance at Finster.

"Ready to give up?" he asked.

"Humph," Finster said indignantly. "You liked what I did with Electricus. What do you think of this?"

None of the tools in Finster's smock *looked* like weapons, but the one he pulled out had a button on the handle, which he squeezed.

"It taps into the entire power supply of this research center!" he explained.

The bolt that shot from the device hit Billy square in the chest. His body didn't go flying; he just collapsed where he was. He wasn't unconscious, but he couldn't move or speak!

His mind still working, Billy tried to figure out what had happened to him. *The human nervous system works with a form of electricity. That shock must have made all my muscles seize. I'm paralyzed!*

Seeing the Blue Ranger frozen on the floor, Goo Fish Junior shivered in anger.

"You're the bad guy! The bad guy!" he shouted at Finster.

Finster looked at Goo Fish Junior. *Another blast from my power tool would paralyze this big fish, too,* he thought. *But with my poor Enhancifier destroyed, Goo Fish Junior is now the* only *way to show Rita Repulsa that my invention ever worked in the first place! The only problem is: How do I get it to act like a monster, not a hero?*

Finster tried to manage a smile. "Did the Blue Ranger tell you that?" he asked. "Well, you shouldn't believe everything you hear. The truth is, *I'm* the one who made you so big and strong."

Goo Fish Junior stood still and blinked. "You did?" he asked.

"Yes! You and I should have a little talk," Finster replied.

Though he couldn't move, Billy heard everything. *No!* he thought. *Don't listen to him!*

But even though Goo Fish Junior now understood human language, he couldn't read Billy's mind. There was nothing the Blue Ranger could do other than watch as Goo Fish Junior tilted his fish body at a slight angle, in a way that made him look curious.

"What do you want to talk about?" the big goldfish asked Finster.

Chapter 15

Good, good, good! Finster thought as he excitedly clapped his hands. *The Blue Ranger will be paralyzed for at least a few minutes, so here's my chance to turn things around.*

Trying to seem friendly, even though he wasn't quite sure how, the alien inventor stepped closer to the big goldfish and patted him on the side. He gave him his widest grin and said, "I'm not the bad guy. Far from it! I'm your friend. That Blue Ranger lying there, *he's* the bad guy! If it were up to him, you'd probably have been a prisoner in that tiny fishbowl for your whole life. Not me, though. I want you to be free! With me, you could have all the world's oceans to swim in!"

Goo Fish Junior wriggled uncomfortably. "The ocean has salt water. I can't breathe in salt water," he said.

Good for you! Billy thought. *You remembered!*

But Finster didn't seem to care. "You're a smart

one, aren't you?" he said. "Well, a nice, big lake then, one that's as large as an ocean. How about that?"

Goo Fish happily bounced on his feet. "Yes, please!"

Finster went on. "What else do goldfish like? Castles? I'll put a great big castle right in the middle for you, with all the food you can eat."

Being hungry all the time, hearing that made the large goldfish very excited. "Food! Food!" he said.

But then, remembering again what Billy had said, he stopped. "I love food, but too much is bad for me, isn't it?"

Finster moved easily from one lie to another. "Nonsense!" he said. "Someone only told you that because they didn't want you to be happy!"

Goo Fish Junior blinked his big round eyes. "They didn't?" he asked.

"No," Finster said. He pointed at himself and added, "But I do!"

He blinked again. "You do?"

Uh-oh, Billy thought. *His hunger takes up most of his goldfish brain. He can't resist!*

Goo Fish Junior, after thinking about it, started rubbing against Finster like a happy dog.

"Friend! Friend!" Goo Fish Junior said.

The slime felt uncomfortable, but Finster kept smiling and tried to pet him again.

This is terrible! Billy thought. *I've got to do something!*

He fought to get his muscles to move, any muscle. Even though his shocked body didn't want to obey, he kept at it.

"I am your friend, your only friend," Finster said. "And as your friend, there's one little thing I want you to do for me." He pointed a furry finger at Billy. "Destroy the Blue Ranger!"

But then Finster gasped. The Blue Ranger had started to move again.

"That's impossible!" he said. "No one can recover that quickly!"

Billy was still groggy and his body ached, but despite the pain, he got to his feet.

"A Power Ranger can," he said.

Not knowing what a Power Ranger was, the big goldfish stomped toward him, saying, "Destroy! Destroy! Destroy!"

Hoping to make him understand, Billy started to gently speak. "Goo Fish Junior—"

But it was too late. He saw a flash of goldfish tail.

THWAM!

The Blue Ranger hit the heavy Plexiglas of the tank containing the large dolphin. For a moment, he looked as if he was stuck there by the moisture. Then his body made a squeaking sound as it slid down to the concrete floor.

Now Billy's muscles didn't only ache from the shock Finster had given him, but they also ached from the new bruises.

Goo Fish Junior clenched his fists. "I can eat all I want!" he said.

"But that will hurt you!" Billy insisted.

"No, it won't!" Goo Fish Junior said. He stepped closer, then turned sideways to make it easier for him to hit the Blue Ranger again.

Still dazed, Billy definitely did not want to take another blow from that tail. He spotted his Power Lance lying nearby.

As the tail came at him, the Blue Ranger grabbed the Power Lance and used it to block the blow.

When his tail hit the lance, Goo Fish Junior screamed, *"Agh!"*

Billy tried to be as gentle as he could, but the

goldfish had never encountered that kind of resistance before. It didn't hurt so much as it surprised him. It also made him very angry.

He shook his fist and stomped his feet. "Destroy! Destroy!" he said.

The Blue Ranger backed up, but Goo Fish Junior kept trying to hit him. Billy had no choice but to keep using his Power Lance to deflect the swiping tail.

And that made the creature madder and madder!

Finster cheered on his creation. "That's it! That's it!" he said. "I'll make the perfect monster out of you yet!"

Chapter 16

A good distance from the tanks and the battle between Billy Cranston and the former subject of his science experiment, the students were having much better luck with their fight against the Putty Patrol.

Thanks to the glue, stink bombs, and flash firecrackers, the simpleminded monsters had no idea which way to turn. They tried to fight back, but wound up hitting one another much more than they did anything else. Disorganized to begin with, the clay-faced foot soldiers were even more scattered and helpless!

"We're doing it!" Ira proudly said as he threw another stink bomb.

Pouring more glue onto the ground, Alani agreed. "Not only did we stand up to those bullies, we're actually helping the Blue Ranger!"

And they were helping—until Bulk and Skull ran back in.

"Eeep!" Skull said when he saw the fight. "We must have gotten turned around!"

"I told you this was the wrong way!" Bulk said.

They tried to stop, but before they could, they hit the oily part of the floor.

Skull slid along, finally stumbling to a stop in front of some canisters that were so tall they stretched to the ceiling. They were connected to a thick hose that was used to put clean water into the tanks.

Bulk had a much harder time stopping. Just as Skull managed to turn to head back, Bulk ran into him. Together, they crashed into the controls for the water canisters, accidentally flipping a lever.

The thick hose filled and then splashed them with a gushing stream of water. It knocked them to the floor. They tried to get back up, but the hose was pointed right at them. The force kept them off balance, so they lay there, soaked and sputtering, as the water kept flowing. Soon it covered the entire floor.

Seeing it, Ira realized what would happen. "Watch out, everyone!" he warned. "That water will melt the glue!"

"I knew we should have used a stronger formula," Randal said. "But who knew we'd be using it on terrifying monsters, not bullies?"

As the water flowed along the floor, not only did it melt the glue, it drenched the students and the rest of their makeshift pranks, making them useless.

Fortunately, Bulk and Skull still couldn't stand up.

Unfortunately, once the smelly smoke and bright flashes cleared, the Putty Patrol realized they were free and ran toward the students!

A terrified Randal grabbed Ira around the wrist and screamed, "Now what do we do?"

Ira, trying to pry his friend free, gave what he thought was the obvious answer:

"Lose, I guess!"

Chapter 17

Back among the tanks, the angry Goo Fish Junior came at the Blue Ranger, swinging his big, deadly tail this way and that. The Blue Ranger kept stepping back, ducking, or blocking the blows with his Power Lance.

Every time the Power Lance touched Goo Fish Junior, no matter how gently, the goldfish became more upset.

"You hurt me!" Goo Fish Junior cried.

"I don't want to hurt you. I'm trying *not* to, but you have to listen to me!" Billy pleaded. "Finster said he would set you free, but he works for an evil space witch named Rita Repulsa. Together they're planning to take over the entire planet and make everyone their slaves, including you!"

"*Ahhh!* Too many words!" the goldfish shouted. Frustrated, Goo Fish Junior tried to grab his head with his hands, but his arms were too short to reach. "What's a witch? What's a Rita Repulsa? What's a planet?!"

Billy backed up farther. Realizing he was trying to explain too much at once, he said, "Let me try to make it simple."

"No!" Goo Fish Junior howled. "No more talk! I don't like to talk!"

Rather than hit the Blue Ranger with his tail, the man-size fish swatted a heavy cart full of scientific equipment. It soared into the air like a big cannonball, heading right at Billy. At the last minute, he knocked it aside with his lance.

With so many things flying around that might hit him, Finster decided to watch from a safer distance. The dog-faced alien couldn't hear exactly what the Blue Ranger and his Enhancified monster were saying to each other, but with all the backing up and ducking the Ranger was doing, one thing seemed perfectly clear.

Goo Fish Junior is winning the fight! he thought. *That makes this the perfect time to contact my wicked queen, Rita!*

Finster grabbed the communicator that hung among the tools on his smock. Like the teleporter, he'd used a combination of magic and alchemy to protect it from the solar flares.

Certain that it would work, he flipped it on and said, "My queen? Your most horribleness?"

Rita Repulsa's drowsy voice answered. "Finster? Where the heck are you? This better be good; you woke me from my nap!"

"Oh, it is good, your wickedness! It's *very* good!" Finster said. "Excellent, in fact, your excellency, so excellently excellent that I can barely contain myself!"

"Get to the point!" Rita snapped. "My head hurts!"

"Yes, your dreadfulness, of course!" Finster said. "If you'll just walk over to the observation balcony and point your long-range telescope at the Marine Island Research Center on Earth, you'll see my latest and, if I may say so myself, *greatest* creation, beating the dickens out of a Power Ranger!"

"What? Where?" Rita said. She already sounded excited. "Oh, I've got it. There you are! What is that, a goldfish? Kind of slimy, isn't it? Oh, who cares? It's trouncing the Blue Power Ranger! Finster, you brilliant devil, how could I ever doubt you? My headache is gone!"

Finster was so relieved, he exhaled in relief. "Thank you, your badness, thank you! Your approval is all I ever—"

Rita cut him off. "Oh, shut up, Finster, and let me watch!"

When Goo Fish Junior's tail hurled a heavy barrel of fish food into the air and the Ranger ducked again, Rita Repulsa cackled.

But her face soured when the Blue Ranger advanced. "I'm sorry. I can't let you hurt anyone else!"

Nearing Goo Fish Junior, he threw himself onto the floor and rolled into his former pet's stubby feet. Goo Fish Junior threw up his arms and fell backward.

Dazed and nearly unconscious, it would be easy now for the Blue Ranger to tie him up and keep him under control.

But Rita had other ideas. "Finster, you know what this calls for?" she asked.

Finster didn't have to guess. He knew what she was thinking. "Using your wand to make my creation supersize?" he asked.

"Exactly!" Rita answered. "Magic wand, make that monster grow!"

Although the Moon Palace, being on the moon, was very far away, the wand's magic allowed it to travel the great distance in an instant. Crashing through the building's domed skylight, it bathed Goo Fish Junior in a sorcerous glow.

Recognizing that glow, the Blue Ranger knew what would happen next. *No!* he thought. *How can I save Goo Fish Junior and the research center now?*

At first, the glow frightened and confused Goo Fish Junior. After all, he'd already been through a lot. When the Enhancifier made him grow the first time, breaking his bowl and leaving him stuck in that small lab room, it was very uncomfortable. But there was a lot more room here. As he grew again, and kept growing, and everything around him got smaller and smaller—he started to enjoy it.

"Whee!" he said. "I'm not just getting bigger, I feel like I'm getting a little smarter!"

Thrilled, Finster pointed once again at the Blue Ranger and said, "Destroy!"

But Goo Fish Junior's booming voice answered, "No!"

Hearing that, Billy smiled. "Then you're on my side again!"

But the still-growing Goo Fish Junior again said, "No!"

Both Finster and Billy furrowed their brows and craned their necks to look up.

"I don't understand," the Blue Ranger said.

"Whose side are you on?" Finster asked.

"Mine!" Goo Fish Junior answered.

Chapter 18

Goo Fish Junior had grown so large that the dorsal fin on his long back actually touched the 150-foot-tall domed ceiling. He looked way down at Billy and Finster. They seemed so tiny, as if *they* were the goldfish and he was the human.

So why should I listen to them? he thought.

"I'm tired of not knowing who to trust," he told them. "From now on, I'm just going to trust myself and fight everyone!"

His body now stretched halfway across the vast space. It only took a single swish of his gargantuan tail to hit both the Blue Ranger, who was pretty close, and the whole Putty Patrol, which was pretty far away.

THWACK!

They all splatted against the same wall, like heavy raindrops.

The tail barely missed Finster and the students, surprising them.

"Well, that was unexpected!" Finster said.

The monster was so big now that whenever Goo Fish Junior moved, even a little, the entire building shook. Terrified, the cowardly Finster ran off. The students had seen what that big tail had done to the Blue Ranger and the Putty Patrol. They still wanted to help, but they also realized they couldn't possibly hope to fight that huge monster. So they ran off, too.

The only people left in sight were Bulk and Skull. They were still flopping in the gushing stream of water from the hose, trying to stand.

Noticing them, Goo Fish Junior tilted his head down for a closer look.

"I know you!" he said.

A single step put one of his big feet on the hose, stopping the flow of water. Bulk and Skull could stand at last. Dripping wet, they'd been temporarily blinded by the rushing water. Despite all the noise, they hadn't seen exactly what had happened, and were planning to go back to running away from the students. Once they wiped their eyes and saw the huge foot on the hose, though, the bullies froze, too terrified to move.

The colossal fish kneeled a little and scooped up Skull in his hand. "You fed me!" he said happily.

"Help!" Skull screamed. "Help, Bulk!"

"Sss-sorry!" Bulk called back. He looked as if he really was. Skull was his only friend, but Bulk was no hero. He'd never even really fought anyone, let alone a giant. Plus, he was still too scared to move.

Goo Fish Junior raised the squirming Skull up to one of his enormous fish eyes.

"You fed me a lot!" he said. "That makes me like you!"

The grip was slimy and uncomfortable, but hearing that the monster liked him made Skull feel better.

"Yeah, yeah! I did feed you a lot," Skull said. "So does that mean I'm, like, your master now? And you'll, like, do whatever I say?"

For the first time, Goo Fish Junior laughed. Becoming giant had really lifted the fish's mood.

"No, no," the huge creature said. "But I will keep you as a pet!"

"Wait . . . what?" Skull said, no longer feeling quite so good.

As the great fish stretched, his fin burst through the domed skylight. The building shook so much that earthquake alarms went off all across the island. As pieces of glass fell from the broken skylight, the Blue

Ranger dove toward Bulk, pushing him out of the way.

But the monster's stretch had damaged more than the skylight. Out in the halls, Billy saw research scientists and staff running as falling bits of plaster rained down around them.

I need help, Billy thought. *Badly.*

He looked at his wrist-communicator. The signal strength had increased like crazy!

But how? he wondered. Then he figured it out. *Whatever Finster used to enhance Goo Fish Junior also enhanced my experiment! The wrist-communicator is designed to piggyback on any signals available nearby, so it's using that. But is it enough to get through the solar flares and reach the others?*

"Jason? Zack? Anyone?" the Blue Ranger said.

He heard a crackly voice answer, "Billy, what's up?"

"Jason! Thank goodness!" the Blue Ranger said. "Finster and Rita have unleashed a giant monster here at the center. Unfortunately, they used Goo Fish Junior to create it!"

"We'll get there as soon as we can," the Red Ranger said, "but you'll have to deal with things on your own for a little while. Those solar flares are still interfering with the teleporter!"

"That makes sense," Billy said. "Finster's device may have enhanced my communication equipment along with Goo Fish Junior, but that wouldn't change the Command Center teleporter."

He thought about it for a moment. "Finster's alchemical tech, that's it! That must be how he teleported here in spite of the solar storm. Zordon, is there anything like that you can use on your end?"

As they spoke, everything began to shake. Uncomfortable with all the walls that surrounded him, Goo Fish Junior was pushing his way through the building.

Zordon's deep voice answered. "I'm afraid I can't help, Billy. Being trapped in a time warp prevents me from interacting with your reality. But we'll keep trying. In the meantime, I have faith that you can handle this until the others arrive."

Slack-jawed, Billy looked around. Goo Fish Junior seemed to be trying to avoid any damage to the tanks, maybe because he felt some kinship with his fellow marine creatures. The rest of the center wasn't as lucky—the giant was tearing apart entire walls and support beams!

Debris fell everywhere. Through the missing

walls, he could see panicked staff and students trying to find the way out.

"Where do I start?" Billy asked.

"With the people," team leader Jason said. "Your first priority is to get everyone to safety! Billy, you can do it!"

Hearing the confidence in Jason's voice gave the Blue Ranger more of his own.

"Right!" Billy said.

Raising his crackling Power Lance to attract everyone's attention, he began shouting. "Everyone, this way! Form an organized group and follow me!"

"You heard the man!" Ira said.

As the building continued to shake, a crowd gathered around the Blue Ranger. Among them, Billy spotted Dr. Anton Fent, the head of the research center. The day had been so busy, Billy hadn't had the chance to speak to the famous scientist in person, or thank him, but he immediately recognized his face from the website and his textbooks on marine life.

"Doctor, what's the safest place on the island?" the Blue Ranger asked.

Like many of the others, the famous scientist had a very hard time keeping his eyes off the huge goldfish destroying his facility. Understanding the danger, he forced himself to focus.

Shaken, he stuttered a bit as he answered. "There's a s-storm bunker o-outside, built in c-case of tropical storms. It can withstand a h-h-hurricane!"

The Blue Ranger nodded. "Perfect!"

Every minute they stayed inside was another minute someone might be crushed by falling pieces of the building, but the main entrance was blocked by debris. Billy had to lead them through the shaking building until they reached a fire door.

Once they were all outside, no longer surrounded by dangerous, crumbling wreckage, they were able to pick up speed, crossing the plaza and heading toward the beach.

When the bunker door was visible, the Blue Ranger waved everyone toward it.

"Whatever you hear," he told them, "stay put until I come back and tell you that it's safe."

Dr. Fent stood by the bunker door, counting people in an effort to make sure no one was left behind. The others all rushed in, except one.

A worried Bulk stopped. He swallowed nervously and said, "Power Ranger, I've got to help save Skull."

Despite all Bulk had done, Billy found his concern for his friend touching.

"I understand," the Blue Ranger replied. "I'll take care of him, I promise. But you've got to get inside with the rest."

Bulk did as he was asked.

When the door to the bunker closed, Billy turned back toward the main building. As he watched, the enormous Goo Fish Junior tore through the last few feet of wall and emerged into the open air.

Billy wanted to ask his teammates for more advice, but his wrist-communicator only gave off static. *I'm not close enough to the Enhancified Goo Fish Junior anymore for my communication experiment to boost the signal,* he realized.

But Billy also realized that he didn't need Jason or the others to tell him what the next step was. It was time for the Blue Ranger to summon his Dinozord, one of the amazing battle vehicles given to the Mighty Morphin Power Rangers by Zordon. Each one was linked to the prehistoric beast symbolizing its power.

"Triceratops, Dinozord Power!" he commanded.

Chapter 19

"Destroy! Destroy!" the immense goldfish cried.

Meanwhile, Finster was so panicked, he didn't think to use his teleporter. Instead he ran as fast as he could, trying to escape the thundering footsteps. Finster wasn't sure if Goo Fish Junior wanted to step on him specifically, or if he just wanted to squash everything in general.

I might think that was a wonderful quality for a monster, Finster thought, *if I weren't in the way!*

On the other hand, when Rita Repulsa started screaming through Finster's communicator, the alien inventor knew exactly whom she was angry with.

"Finster!" she shrieked. "What's going on? Are you actually being chased by your own monster? Why'd it swat my Putty Patrol? And what in blazes did you mean by running off like that without telling me in the first place?"

Her voice took on a very special tone when she

was this angry with him. It was sort of a cross between nails on a blackboard and the squeal of a dentist's drill. Worse, the distraction slowed down Finster at a time when slowing down was not a good idea. A big fish foot was about to come down right on top of him! Finster leaped as far as his squat legs could take him. The foot flattened a tall palm tree behind and to the left of him.

"Uh . . . which question shall I answer first, your frightfulness?" Finster asked.

"All of them!" Rita yelled.

At the same time, Goo Fish Junior cried out, "Destroy! Destroy!"

Finster was suddenly covered by a foot-shaped shadow.

Oh my! he thought. *Maybe he* is *after me!*

Desperate, he ran and, again, barely escaped in time.

Finster hoped Rita wouldn't be upset by the short delay in his response. Then again, he knew she wasn't going to be happy about what he had to tell her, no matter *when* he said it.

He swallowed and spoke. "I'm afraid, my queen, he's gone rogue!"

"Rogue?!" Rita repeated. She was so full of rage, it felt as if her voice had somehow reached through the communicator and slapped Finster. "No one goes rogue without my permission!" she said. "I can't have my commands disobeyed! It's bad for morale! *My* morale!"

The evil minion tried to laugh at Rita's joke, since he knew that pleased her, but he was too busy running. Up ahead, he saw a supply shed.

That looks sturdy, he thought. *Maybe I can hide in there.*

"Destroy! Destroy!" the monster howled.

His foot came down ahead of Finster, crushing the shed completely.

I guess not, Finster thought.

"Finster!" Rita screamed. "I'm going to make an example of you! Until you get that oversize carp under control somehow, I'm casting a spell to take away your teleporter privileges! You're on your own!"

Finster gulped. She'd never done *that* before.

"On my own?" he said. "No teleporting?"

But she didn't answer. The communicator had gone dead.

This is the worst of the worst! Finster thought. *Rita*

might be making an example out of me, but Goo Fish Junior will make a pancake out of me!

As he scurried for his life, Finster had to admit that, for the first time, he deeply wished his invention hadn't worked quite so well.

Chapter 20

Like all the Zords, the Blue Ranger's Triceratops Dinozord would hear his call no matter where he was. Their connection was based on powerful alien technology, so the solar flares wouldn't stop it, either. Among the high dunes of the far-off desert where it stayed, the powerful vehicle, a sort of living machine, instantly responded. Able to teleport to any part of the world, it rolled up on the shore of the tropical island moments later.

As Billy watched, its dual tank treads kicked up a great spray of sand. The cockpit from which he could pilot the battle machine sat right behind the heavily armored sensors that resembled the head of the three-horned dinosaur. Using his enhanced strength, the Blue Ranger made the high leap and settled in behind the controls.

He was ready for action!

The metallic blue of the Dinozord sparkled in the

sun. Seeing it, the giant Goo Fish Junior, still holding Skull in one hand, swung toward it and narrowed his eyes.

Looks like I've got his attention, Billy thought. *Maybe I can lead him to an uninhabited part of the island until the other Power Rangers get here.*

Together, the five Zords had the ability to combine into the Dino Megazord. The Megazord would stand every bit as tall as the massive fish and had the power of an army. The Triceratops Dinozord was impressive, but barely came up to Goo Fish Junior's torso.

Goo Fish Junior eyed the Dinozord for a bit, then turned and headed back toward the main building. The sleek, modern facility was now in shambles—mostly because of the Goo Fish Junior–size hole the monster had made on his way out. Huge chunks of concrete lay in heaps around it.

As the gigantic goldfish walked away, he kept his back to Billy.

What's he up to? the Blue Ranger wondered.

It didn't take long to find out. Once the monster was close enough, he used his tail to swat a large mass of concrete, half the size of the Dinozord, into the air.

Looking like a huge asteroid from outer space, it

came flying at top speed right at Billy.

The Triceratops Dinozord might not be as big as the giant fish, but it had a few tricks of its own. Among them was its main weapon: the dual laser cannons.

Thinking fast, Billy aimed and fired. The two searing beams hit the concrete mass dead center. It exploded in midair, tumbling down on the island in small pieces.

"Got it!" the Blue Ranger cried.

But there was a problem. Even though the pieces were small, they were heavy. Some battered the outside of the bunker that sheltered the students and scientists, denting its walls.

Billy realized the danger at once. *If Goo Fish Junior keeps that up, those falling rocks could demolish the bunker by accident! I've got to get between him and the bunker so he focuses his attacks on me.*

He deftly maneuvered the cockpit controls. The heavy treads of the Dinozord turned, moving the Blue Ranger closer to the monster. Before Billy could get the battle machine in front of the bunker, though, the colossal goldfish turned around and stomped off. At first Billy thought he might be running away, but when Goo Fish Junior reached the main building he stopped.

Once he was there, he placed Skull on a section of the roof that was still intact.

"You'll be safe there, my pet!" he said.

"Wait, what?" Skull shouted, looking around. "But I'm afraid of heights!"

"Do you want me to put you somewhere else?" the big fish asked.

The thought of being held again in that slimy, giant grip made Skull's eyes go wide.

"No, no!" he said. "This is fine! It's great, even! Just leave me here, please!"

Goo Fish Junior tilted as if nodding. Looking down, the big fish noticed the transparent wall he and Billy had seen when he first arrived on the island. The large dolphin was swimming on the other side. The monster looked as if he was thinking about something.

I guess it's a good thing he wanted to keep Skull safe, Billy thought. *But what's he doing now?*

Suddenly, Goo Fish Junior bent over. Using both hands, the giant tore out the transparent tank wall. Thousands and thousands of gallons of salt water rushed onto the plaza, along with the large dolphin! Carried by the water from the tank, the great animal rolled over and over across the plaza. Finally the large dolphin settled, surprised but unharmed, in one of the shallow open-air pools in front of the building.

Billy knew that, as a mammal, the large dolphin could breathe in the air. He also knew it needed water to support its weight and keep its body temperature cool. It could live for a few hours, but after that, it would need a lot more water to stay healthy.

"Sorry, Goo Fish Junior," the Blue Ranger said to himself. "Skull is safe now, but there are other lives at stake. I can't take it easy on you anymore."

With a sigh, he aimed the dual laser cannons directly at the monster and fired. Billy was hoping to knock him out, or at least push him away from the tanks and pools. As it turned out, Goo Fish Junior was surprisingly fast for a giant goldfish.

Still holding the Plexiglas wall, Goo Fish Junior raised it up as a shield. The rays from the cannons glanced off the surface and shot harmlessly into the air.

The move looked really familiar to Billy.

Huh, he thought. *That's almost the same way Electricus used mirrors to deflect my blaster. Goo Fish Junior was in his bowl at the time, so he saw that fight. Did Finster's Enhancifier also enhance his memory? It's a shame that creepy alien doesn't use his powers for good!*

Considering his next move, Billy edged the Dinozord closer, but then things got even stranger. Seeing the dolphin lying in the pool, Goo Fish Junior headed for it. Billy worried he might try to hurt it, but he was too close to the dolphin to risk another shot—he might hit the dolphin by accident.

Surprisingly, the goldfish didn't attack the dolphin. Instead, opening his incredibly enormous fish mouth, he leaned down to suck half the water out of the pool.

Not sure what to expect next, Billy carefully moved the Dinozord even closer, so he'd be ready to respond no matter what happened. But then Goo Fish Junior lifted up the dolphin in his arms and started carrying it to the shore. As he did, the monster let some of the salt water he'd sucked up stream out of his mouth, keeping the large mammal moist and comfortable.

Billy was fascinated.

I guess he does *feel a connection to other creatures that live in the water,* he thought. *They're probably not as confusing to him as people are. It must have been hard for him to hear different things from me and Finster so soon after being able to understand any words in the first place. I guess I can get why he decided not to trust either of us. Deep down, he's still a simple fish, and ignoring what he didn't understand was the easiest thing to do.*

Billy followed inside his Dinozord but kept his distance. Goo Fish Junior, carrying the dolphin like a huge baby, reached the shore and kept going until he was knee-deep in the ocean. Considering his giant height, that was pretty deep.

And then he gently let the large dolphin go.

Once it swam off, though, anything gentle about the big goldfish disappeared. Suddenly, Goo Fish Junior was very angry again. He started stomping his huge feet and sending high waves crashing into the shore. Billy didn't understand what had changed his mood so fast, until the monster started screaming.

"I want to go, too! I want to go, too!" Goo Fish Junior said. "But I can't breathe in the salt water. I can only hold it in my mouth!"

Despite the damage he'd done, Billy felt a lot of sympathy for the fish. After all, it hadn't chosen to become a monster. Hoping he might still be able to reach him, Billy spoke through the Dinozord's speaker system.

"Goo Fish Junior, let me help you!" he said.

"Maybe I can figure out how to shrink you back down and—"

The frustrated goldfish cut him off. "No! I don't trust you!" he said. "You just shot at me!"

That made sense, too. Why *should* he trust the Blue Ranger?

Goo Fish Junior was smart, but he also got frustrated very easily. Like a child having a tantrum, he stomped harder and harder, making the waves rise and rise. Still upset, he started kicking, sending up tons of sand and rock from the ocean floor along with the water. The island's small dock started to shake. Worse, Goo Fish Junior was stomping back toward the shore!

Hoping to stop him while he was still far away from the bunker, the Blue Ranger decided to use the Dinozord's second weapon.

"Chain-link power cables!" Billy called as he activated them.

The Triceratops Dinozord's two large side horns shot away from its forehead. They were attached to two massive, electrified cables that followed the horns as they flew through the air. Billy had used the power cables to shock and subdue many foes. Once they struck, they remained attached to the Dinozord, so he could use them to drag a monster down and even tie it up.

But when Goo Fish Junior saw them coming, he did something unexpected. Instead of trying to get out of the way, he leaned forward and spat salt water he'd sucked up from the pool. The heavy rush of water pushed the power cables back the way they had come.

At first the Blue Ranger thought his attack had simply failed—but it was worse than that. The water, and the cables, kept coming—until they hit the Dinozord with incredible force. With a horribly bright flash, the electricity meant for the monster shot through Billy and the battle tank instead, frying the controls. At the same time, the blast of water lifted the Zord from the ground and sent it crashing sideways into a seawall that was meant to keep the buildings safe from high storm tides.

Paralyzed by the electric shock, Billy felt himself hurled from the cockpit. He landed on the beach, barely conscious. As the water receded, he glimpsed his upended Dinozord. Still smoking and crackling, it seemed useless.

And so was Billy. His eyelids fluttered. He was still awake, but the bright flash had hurt his eyes. He had to close them. The last thing he saw was the angry Goo Fish Junior towering behind the damaged Triceratops Dinozord. After that, the Blue Ranger only heard the giant's heavy, pounding feet and the loud crashes and bangs as it created more destruction.

But then Billy felt hands on his shoulders.

Someone was trying to pull him out of danger!

Too weak to speak or open his eyes, he desperately hoped his fellow Power Rangers had arrived.

Jason? Trini? Is it you? he thought.

If not, Goo Fish Junior would continue his rampage unopposed.

Chapter 21

The sand against the Blue Ranger's back didn't feel too bad as he was dragged along the beach. Soon, though, whoever was pulling him took him across some much less comfortable concrete. Billy was already so hurt and groggy that he didn't have the strength to say anything about it. When he was pulled up some very steep steps, and across what felt like a lot of extremely uncomfortable rocks, he still couldn't speak.

Along the way, though, Billy realized his rescuer couldn't be one of his fellow Power Rangers. Jason, Zack, Trini, or Kimberly would definitely have said something by now.

Could it be Ira, Alani, or one of the other students? Or the scientists? he wondered. *I hope they're not putting themselves in danger.*

Despite his bruises, the Blue Ranger's enhanced suit helped him recover quickly. While he still hurt from the crash, in no time he was able to open his eyes and finally see who had saved him.

It was quite a surprise.

"Finster?" Billy gasped. "You?"

The inventor was hovering right over him! Hard as it was to believe, Rita Repulsa's trusted minion had actually dragged him to safety. The Blue Ranger instinctively tried to back-crawl to get away, but his bruises kept him from moving much. Finster frowned and gave the Blue Ranger some space.

They were in the ruins of the main building. The electricity was out, making it dark and cool, but they were sheltered by what was left of the walls and the ceiling. The dog-faced alien must have pulled Billy there all the way from the beach.

No wonder he didn't say anything, the Blue Ranger thought.

Even now, Finster didn't look like he knew what he should say. He waddled around the wreckage in silence, then started to pace. He rubbed his hands together nervously, glancing over at the shocked Blue Ranger now and then, and shook his head.

He seemed just as surprised as Billy by what he'd done.

Finally, Finster said, "Yes, yes! I know! But I think

if you look at the situation logically, most people would realize that given the situation, it was the only thing I *could* do." He stopped pacing and looked up at the sky beyond the broken roof, worried. "Not Rita, though, she wouldn't realize that at all. But she's not most people, is she? Oh no! If she ever finds out . . ."

A confused Billy forced himself into a half-sitting position. "What are you talking about? Why would you save my life?"

Finster clenched his fists. "You're asking the wrong question!" he said. "It's not about saving *your* life! If it was, you'd still be out there! Seeing a Power Ranger destroyed would be my second favorite thing ever. The problem is that my number *one* favorite thing is saving *my* life! After being almost stepped on by my own monster three times, it dawned on me that you and I have something . . . I'm not sure how to say this, it's very difficult, as you can imagine, but here goes . . ." Finster took a deep breath before finishing his sentence. "We have something in common."

Billy stiffened and again tried to crawl away. "Us? You and me?" he said. "Something in common?"

Finster nodded. "Terrible, isn't it? But that goldfish is completely out of control! And as long as it's stomping around following its own orders, Rita has magically blocked me from teleporting back to the Moon Palace!"

The Blue Ranger frowned. "I'm not going to help you get Goo Fish Junior under your control!" he said firmly.

Finster shivered and growled. "I didn't think you would! But I also assume you'd rather he *didn't* demolish this island and everyone on it. So I'm guessing you *would* want to help turn him back into a normal goldfish. Wouldn't you? Am I wrong? *Please* tell me I'm not wrong."

Billy looked through the huge holes in the wall. Outside, on the beach, he could see Goo Fish Junior tearing out the tall palm trees and hurling them every which way.

As he threw tree after tree, the enormous goldfish shouted, "I hate this tree! And this one! And especially *this* tree!"

Once the palm trees that were in reach of his giant hands were gone, Goo Fish Junior began doing the same thing with pieces of the concrete seawall, picking them up and hurling them. The childish tantrum seemed like it could go on for hours—or at least as long as anything on the island remained standing.

And that included the bunker where the students and scientists were hiding!

I have no idea how soon the other Power Rangers will get here, Billy thought. *By then, it could be too late. I have to protect the island somehow.*

Billy looked back at Finster and sighed. "You're right," he said. "I have to stop him no matter what."

Finster shook his head. "Not just you," he said. "*We* have to stop him. So, you admit that just in this one, teeny-tiny situation, we have a common goal?"

The Blue Ranger thought about it. "I suppose we do. If we declare a truce, we could work together to stop him."

Finster nodded. "It would be completely temporary, of course. I, for one, will pretend it never happened," he said.

When he started fishing in his smock, Billy tensed, expecting a trick. He only relaxed when Finster held up the broken Enhancifier.

The Blue Ranger stared at it. "With some repairs and alterations, your device can be used in reverse, turning Goo Fish Junior back to normal!"

"I could repair the Enhancifier myself if I could

get back to my workshop, but as I just explained, I'm stuck here," Finster said. He lowered his head in shame. "You, unfortunately, know the Earth equipment better than I do."

"I never thought I'd say this, but I guess we're agreed," the Blue Ranger said. He put out his hand.

Finster turned up his nose and said, "No reason to be ridiculous about it!"

A whiny voice shouted at them from above. "You gotta do something!" the voice pleaded.

The Blue Ranger looked up. It was Skull. He was still standing on the small bit of the building's roof where Goo Fish Junior had placed him.

"That monster wants to keep me as a pet!" Skull cried. "I don't think I'd last long in a goldfish bowl! I mean, how would I even breathe?"

Skull was so loud that both the Blue Ranger and Finster worried about the same thing. They started waving at Skull to be quiet.

"Lower your voice!" Billy said.

"Not so loud!" said Finster.

"What?" Skull shouted. "Why not?"

Unfortunately, Skull soon realized why they were worried. He was up so high, his voice carried all the way to the beach. His shouting had attracted Goo Fish Junior's attention!

"My pet!" the giant cried out happily. "I almost forgot about you!"

"Oh no," Skull whimpered.

The Blue Ranger fought his pain and tried to climb up to save Skull. He was fast, but not as fast as the monster. In just a few pounding steps, the huge creature traveled the distance from the beach to the building.

In a flash, Goo Fish Junior once again snatched up Skull.

Skull whined, "Aw! Couldn't you have forgotten about me for just a little longer?"

The goldfish lifted him near his eye and seemed to smile. "When I was little," he said, "you called me Little Bulky. Now that *you're* little, I'm going to call you Little Skully! Come with me, Little Skully!"

Goo Fish Junior stomped off with his prize. When he nearly stepped on the bunker, the Blue Ranger gasped.

A few yards in the other direction and they would have been crushed! he thought.

Billy climbed back down and looked at Finster.

The idea of working with one of Rita's minions seemed crazy, but he didn't see any other choice.

"Before we start, we have to make some rules," the Blue Ranger said. "I'm not going to leave you with a weapon as dangerous as the Enhancifier!"

"I hadn't thought of that," Finster said. Then he crossed his arms. "But I'm certainly not going to leave *you* with such a magnificent weapon, either! Or *any* weapon for that matter. So what do we do?"

Billy thought about it. "I've got it," he said. "I can install some circuits in it, so that once it's used on Goo Fish Junior, it will self-destruct. That way, no one gets to keep it. Agreed?"

Finster pouted. "But the circuits are from a world that no longer exists! My Enhancifier would be gone forever!" he said.

The ground shook as Goo Fish Junior stomped nearby. A few more pieces of the building fell. Finster squealed and ducked.

"All right! All right! I agree!" Finster said.

"Good," Billy answered. "Then let's get to work before the whole island is destroyed."

Chapter 22

From way up in Goo Fish Junior's fist, Skull had a great view of the whole island, but he didn't like it very much. He kept trying to pull himself free from the slimy grasp, but it was no use.

"What would you like to see me destroy next, Little Skully?" Goo Fish Junior asked.

"Me?" Skull said. Then he realized there was no one else up there the giant fish could be talking to. For that matter, there wasn't anyone else he'd call "Little Skully."

Skull swallowed hard. "*Ulp!* Oh . . . nothing, really," he said. "I'm fine. Maybe . . . maybe you could put me down, and I promise I'll come back later?"

Goo Fish Junior tilted his body left and right as if shaking his head no. It made Skull dizzy.

"I'm sorry, Little Skully," the giant goldfish said. "But everyone says so many different things, it's hard for me to know when they're lying. Even talking about it makes me mad! I'm so angry, I feel like I have to destroy something with my big feet!"

"Do you *have* to?" Skull asked. "It really shakes me up!"

"Yes, yes, I do!" Goo Fish Junior said. He looked around and saw the bunker. "I know! I'll stomp on that!"

As the great fish took a giant step, Skull covered his eyes.

Goo Fish Junior pulled his leg up. He was about to use his tremendous foot to kick in the bunker door, but before he could, he heard a loud rumbling. The rumbling soon got so heavy, it made everything shake.

"Earthquake!" Skull shouted.

"What's an earthquake?" Goo Fish Junior asked.

Skull was too afraid to answer, so the monster turned his wide body toward the sound to see what it was for himself. He was very surprised to see *another* giant rising from the wreckage of the research center!

Goo Fish Junior's big, wide eyes got even bigger and wider when he recognized the blue-and-white uniform the new giant was wearing.

"That looks just like the human who told me that eating too much was bad for me!" the goldfish said.

Skull's eyes got wider, too. "That is *one* big Power Ranger!" he said.

Goo Fish Junior harrumphed. "He's not *that* big," he said.

It was true. Even though the Blue Ranger was giant, he wasn't nearly as tall as Goo Fish Junior. At the same time, the Blue Ranger was still at least four times bigger than any other human that the monster had seen.

As for the giant Billy, he felt like he had at least some idea what the world looked like to the gargantuan monsters he often fought with the Power Rangers.

From up here, it all seems . . . a little smaller, he thought.

When the Blue Ranger and Finster had finished their work on the Enhancifier, they'd realized that its rays would be too small and narrow to completely cover something as big as Goo Fish Junior. To make sure it would work, they'd strapped it on Billy's wrist, and then he'd turned it on himself!

Now that the Blue Ranger *and* the Enhancifier had been enlarged, he was sure the beam would be big enough.

But there was another problem. Finster didn't want a big Power Ranger wandering around all the time, and Billy didn't particularly want to stay giant—so the effect was only temporary. Billy had to finish their plan before he shrank back down.

But if he fired the Enhancifier while Goo Fish Junior was holding Skull, the bully would *also* be hit by the ray. Skull would get so tiny, they might never find him again! The Blue Ranger didn't particularly like Skull, but he didn't want to see him shrink to the size of an ant, either.

Goo Fish Junior likes Little Skully, Billy thought. *Maybe I can talk him into putting him down.*

The Blue Ranger took a few steps closer. He moved slowly so that he didn't seem like too much of a threat. "We never took you out of your bowl and held you like that, Goo Fish Junior," he said. "You should put Little Skully down. Otherwise you might hurt him."

Goo Fish Junior narrowed his big eyes. "No! I remember how you took the food out of my bowl that Little Skully put in, so I couldn't eat it! Now you want him, too, but you can't have him! He's my pet!"

"Please give me to him! Please?" Skull begged.

But the great fish only wrapped his other hand

around Skull, to hold him tighter.

"Oomph!" Skull said.

He remembers everything, Billy thought. *If I'm going to get him to do anything, I have to stop thinking like a human and start thinking like a fish that's always hungry.*

The Blue Ranger looked around. Thanks to the better view his height gave him, he could see very far. Inside the main building, near the tanks, he saw the stacked barrels of fish food kept handy for their marine "guests."

The small krill that they feed the large dolphin aren't the same as the freeze-dried flakes Goo Fish Junior is used to, Billy thought. *But opportunistic feeders go for anything that seems edible. If his appetite has gotten anywhere as big as he is, they just might work.*

"You want food, Goo Fish Junior?" the Blue Ranger called. "I'll get you some food!"

Billy walked over and bent down. When he was normal size, the barrels had seemed pretty big. Now he easily picked one up and pried off the top.

He shook out some of the krill on the ground between himself and Goo Fish Junior.

"Here you go!" he said.

Seeing and smelling the food, the huge fish got very excited. "Food! Food!" he shouted.

In half a step, he was close enough to lean over and suck all the krill into his mouth.

"Mmm!" he said.

"Is the food good?" the Blue Ranger asked.

"It is! It is! Give me more!" the big fish said.

Billy grabbed more barrels. He held as many as he could and ripped another open. This time, he poured the krill out bit by bit, backing up as he did.

If I make a trail leading him away from the bunker, at least everyone there will be safe, Billy thought.

Goo Fish Junior followed along happily. Over and over, he dipped down, ate, and then rose back up to see where the next bit of krill was. All the up and down made Skull feel as if he were on a roller coaster.

"Yeow! I'm too short to go on this ride!" he called.

He was uncomfortable, but not hurt—and Billy's trick was working! Soon they'd left the bunker and the buildings of the research center behind, reaching the part of the island that had been left to nature.

Now if Goo Fish Junior has another tantrum, the only thing he can stomp is palm trees, Billy thought.

The next step is to rescue Skull.

Shortly they reached a big clearing in the palm-tree forest, near the base of the island's only mountain. Goo Fish Junior, having gobbled up the last of the trail, stood up and looked eagerly at Billy, waiting for more food. Skull, meanwhile, looked green, as if he was about to barf from the crazy ride.

"Give me more!" the fish said.

But Billy had only three barrels left. He knew what he had to do now, but he wanted to think it through one more time before he made his move. He didn't want to make a mistake that might hurt Skull.

Even the short wait was enough to make the monster-fish angry. To prove he meant business, Goo Fish Junior stomped his foot so hard, the ground shook. A few boulders rolled down the side of the mountain.

"Okay! Okay!" the Blue Ranger said.

This time, rather than make another trail, Billy ripped open all three of the remaining barrels and poured the krill into one big pile.

I feel a little bad about overfeeding him, the Blue Ranger thought. *Then again, I have no idea how much food it would take to overfeed a giant goldfish!*

When Goo Fisher Junior bent over and began sucking in the krill like a big vacuum cleaner, Billy sprang into action. He raced and jumped up onto the busy monster. After an acrobatic flip, he landed on the creature's shoulder.

The Blue Ranger was big, but the goldfish was still a giant in comparison. Billy felt like a squirrel crawling on a human as he ran along the arm toward the big hand that held Skull.

Goo Fish Junior saw and felt the Blue Ranger, but his hunger was so strong, he was torn between finishing his food and fighting back. That gave Billy the extra time he needed to reach his hand and pry apart the giant fingers.

"Ow!" the big fish shouted. "That hurts!"

The only thing more important than food to the goldfish was stopping the pain—so Goo Fish Junior stood up fast. He was *so* fast that both Billy and Skull were thrown into the air!

Billy wasn't a trained gymnast like the Pink Ranger, Kimberly, but he'd picked up a thing or two. With the help of his enhanced speed and strength, he was able to flip in midair, grab Skull, and land on his feet.

The normal-size Skull was like a toddler in the big Blue Ranger's arms. They looked at each other for a moment, surprised. Billy quickly set him down.

"Get out of here!" the Blue Ranger said.

"No kidding!" Skull said. He ran off.

With Skull safe, all the Blue Ranger had to do was use the modified Enhancifier on Goo Fish Junior. But the fish wasn't quite done being a monster yet.

"You took my pet!" Goo Fish Junior screamed.

Using his enormous tail, he swatted the side of the mountain, causing an avalanche!

Some of the boulders coming down at the Blue Ranger were even bigger than he was! He ducked and rolled, avoiding the biggest rocks, and managed to get back to his feet.

But then Goo Fish Junior spun again, swinging his powerful tail right at the Blue Ranger. Just as that big tail came at him, Billy fired the Enhancifier. Its rays bathed the whole monster in a greenish glow.

It worked! Goo Fish Junior immediately began to get smaller. His shrinking tail missed the Ranger by inches! Once he was nearly normal size, he could no longer breathe in the air.

Billy scooped him up in his hands. "I've got to get

you into some water, as fast as I can!"

But the squirming fish couldn't answer anymore.

All of a sudden, the Enhancifier crackled and popped, completely destroying itself.

That was part of Billy's agreement with Finster. Now neither would have the Enhancifier to use as a weapon. But it also meant that the Blue Ranger's time as a giant was over. He started to shrink, as well!

As fast as he could, Billy raced back toward the research center's wrecked main building. But as he shrank, the length of his strides got shorter and shorter. Would the Blue Ranger make it back in time to save the fish?

Thanks to his enhanced speed, he did. Finding a working water fountain, he grabbed a cup, filled it with freshwater, and put the little Goo Fish Junior inside. The goldfish swirled about in the water, opening and closing his mouth as if he could still talk. Now that Goo Fish Junior was no longer Enhancified, Billy couldn't tell for sure what the fish was trying to say, but he liked to think it was something along the lines of:

"Thank you!"

Tired, Billy set down the cup and started looking

for a larger bowl to place the fish in, so it would be more comfortable.

But it seemed his troubles weren't over yet.

Finster was running toward him with some sort of spear—the truce was over!

Chapter 23

"Aghh! I will destroy you!" Finster cried as he rushed forward, carrying the makeshift spear.

It looked like he'd fashioned the weapon the same way he had Electricus, from pieces of equipment lying around the laboratories. But even though Finster was shouting dramatically, he really wasn't running particularly fast—even for Finster. The weapon also didn't look particularly dangerous, just very shiny.

Is that just a bunch of metal cafeteria trays rolled into a pole and wrapped in wire? Billy thought.

All the Blue Ranger had to do to avoid being hit was calmly turn sideways.

The alien inventor went rushing past. Rather than turn and "attack" again, Finster kept going until he was outside the building.

As he kept running, Finster frantically spoke into his communicator.

"My queen! I've done as you've asked, and I swear

I'll never wander off without your permission again!" he said. "Why, I even attacked the Blue Ranger myself just to prove my loyalty!"

Before Billy could react, the air around him crackled with some very familiar colored streams of light. As four powerful figures stepped from the glowing haze, he felt himself relax. It was his fellow Power Rangers!

"Glad we got here!" Zack said. "There was finally enough of a break in the solar flares for us to get through!"

Spotting the fleeing Finster, Jason, the Red Ranger, pointed.

"Quick!" Jason said. "He's getting away!"

The team raced into action, with Billy in the lead.

The alien inventor was moving as fast as he could, but he was no match for the speed of the Mighty Morphin Power Rangers. The Blue Ranger was soon right behind, reaching out to grab him.

But just then Rita Repulsa's cackling voice came through Finster's communicator. "Ah, I'd leave you stuck down there forever if I didn't need you so badly!" she said. "But I've got a great big heart, and no one else knows how to work your Monster-Matic.

Come on home now, or else!"

Finster began to disappear. But just before he vanished completely, he dropped the spear and gave the Blue Ranger a wink. It was almost as if he was trying to say, *I know very well that my lame attack couldn't do you any real harm. I was only putting on a good front for Rita. But now our deal is over.*

For his part, Billy had to admit it had been interesting working with someone who didn't need his tech-speak translated.

Still, it was clear that the next time they met, it would be as enemies.

The Pink Ranger came to a halt beside Billy and cocked her head.

"Did Finster just . . . *wink* at you?" she asked.

"Long story," Billy said. "A *very* long story."

Zack picked up the spear. "Finster must be losing his touch. This thing is a piece of junk!"

Chapter 24

Tens of thousands of miles away at the Moon Palace, Finster had to admit he was glad to see Rita Repulsa. Even if she was still furious with him, it was great to be home, to see his workshop with all his tools. It was even great to see Rita's crescent-moon-tipped magic wand as she swatted him with it.

WHAP!

It still hurt, though.

"Yeow!" he cried. "What was that for, your malevolence?"

"For sneaking out in the first place!" she said, pulling back for another swing. "And, Finster, just so you know, really the only reason I took you back was to keep you from being captured by those putrid Power Rangers! I couldn't have you blabbing and giving away all my beauty secrets!"

Rather than hit him again, she stretched back and gave off a long, loud cackle. "Ha-aha-ha!"

Despite his relief at being back, Finster's feelings were hurt. "I would *never* have blabbed about anything, your nastiness, I swear!" he said.

"Ah, you already blab too much." She pointed toward his shop. "Now get back to work."

Finster nodded as rapidly as he could. "Yes, your horridness. At once."

She narrowed her eyes at him. "And this time I want a monster that does what we *tell* it to do!"

Finster bowed over and over as he backed into his workshop. "Yes, your mercilessness!" he said. "After studying all those primitive fish tanks down on Earth, I think I've figured out a way to adjust the moisture absorption of the Monster-Matic so we can produce Putty Patrols even faster!"

Rita frowned, waved her long fingernails at Finster, and then turned away. "Moisture what?" she said. "Eh, whatever! Don't tell me about it, just do it!"

"Of course, my queen," Finster said.

He stepped into his workshop and clapped. He patted the Monster-Matic. It hissed cheerfully as if recognizing its master's touch.

The Enhancifier was a wonderful break, but I think I will stick with clay for a while, he thought.

Remembering his destroyed invention, Finster had to admit that, in spite of himself, it had been nice working with someone he didn't have to explain his genius to.

And when it comes to smarts, I have to say the Blue Ranger was no slouch, either. A worthy opponent, he thought.

But then he looked around, worried that Rita Repulsa might somehow hear him thinking. Of course she couldn't. At least he didn't *think* she could.

At any rate, this was Finster's home, and it was time to get back to work.

Clay and gadgets aren't really the point, he told himself. *The only thing that really matters is figuring out how best to demolish the Power Rangers once and for all.*

And then he happily started designing his next monster. He was sure it would be his most monstrous monster yet. He was sure that, this time, it would triumph!

Back at the Marine Island Research Center, the grateful staff and students emerged from the bunker and looked around at the devastation.

Meanwhile, the Power Rangers surrounded Billy.

The Red Ranger was the first to pat him on the back. "You did it, man!" he said.

The Blue Ranger exhaled. "Hey, Jason, believe me, there wasn't a single second that I didn't wish you all were here with me! It would have been much, *much* easier."

"We know," the Black Ranger, Zack, said, grinning. "Still, it must be nice knowing you can face off against Putty Patrols, a giant monster, and Finster all on your own!"

"I wasn't exactly alone," Billy said. He pointed to Ira, Alani, Randal, and the others. "My fellow science students actually stepped up to help fight the Putty Patrol." Before telling his teammates the rest, he hesitated. "And, well, to be completely honest, when the giant Goo Fish Junior went out of control, he nearly beat me."

He nodded sadly at the overturned battle tank on the beach. "He even took out my Triceratops Dinozord."

But Alpha 5 would be able to repair it. Soon enough, the Dinozord would return to its desert home until Billy needed it again.

"Then how'd you beat him?" Kimberly asked curiously.

"I really hate to say this," Billy confessed, "but the fact is, I might not have won if it wasn't for Finster. He had his selfish reasons for it, true, but he saved me."

The Pink Ranger put up her hands. "Wait," she said.

The Red Ranger tapped his helmet near his ears as if he'd misheard. "What?" he said.

The Black Ranger shook his head. "Who?" he asked.

The Yellow Ranger took a step back. "Why?"

Billy nodded. Once they calmed down long enough to listen, he told them what had happened.

They were still stunned when Billy got to what he felt was the most exciting part:

". . . and then all we had to do was reverse engineer the thermionic guns on a dysfunctional electron microscope to replicate the augmentation aspects of the Enhancifier's alien circuitry."

Yellow Ranger Trini explained, "He means they used pieces of a broken microscope to repair Finster's whatsis."

Zack whistled. "Wow," he said. "I thought he just made things out of clay."

The conversation was interrupted when Zordon's voice boomed from their wrist-communicators. "The solar flares have cleared completely!" he announced.

Alpha 5 chirped in, "Billy, why don't you tell us all what happened back here at the Command Center?"

Billy eyed the students and staff. "Actually, Alpha 5, I should probably change back into my civilian clothes to let everyone know I'm still alive!" he said.

The Yellow Ranger shrugged. "Sorry you'll have to take that long water-shuttle ride home."

Billy shook his head. "Oh, I don't mind," he said. "We weren't together long, but I'd kind of like to take the time to say goodbye to everyone."

Trini smiled approvingly. "So quiet Billy Cranston made some new friends, after all, huh? You're full of surprises."

"Just don't go making friends with any more of Rita's minions!" Zack joked.

"Ha!" Billy said. "That's *not* something you have to worry about."

"Aye-yi-yi!" Alpha 5 said. "What's he talking about, Billy?"

"We'll fill you and Zordon in when we get back," Jason said. "Meanwhile, Billy's going to take a well-earned break."

A few hours later, Billy, having cleaned his lab as best he could, was back in his street clothes and heading toward the docks. He carried a small bowl with the restored Goo Fish Junior along with what was left of the rest of his belongings.

Although the students had all arrived at different times, they were heading home together. It made the water shuttle a little crowded, but Billy didn't mind. Between all the packing and cleaning, he hadn't had much of a chance to speak to anyone yet.

As Ira moved to make space for him, Billy noticed how exhausted everyone looked—and with good reason.

"Everyone all right?" Billy asked.

"A little shaken," Randal, the usually nervous student, said. "But we're all here and we're all okay, thanks to the Blue Ranger. We were a little worried about you, though!"

"That's right, Billy," Alani said. "You never told us where you were during the big fight. All I know is that you weren't in the bunker!"

Billy shrugged. "It's not a very exciting story. I didn't make it out in time, so the Blue Ranger took me to a spot in the basement. It was dark and, I admit, a little scary, but here I am, safe and sound." Feeling a little emotional, he cleared his throat. "We haven't known one another long, but I'm going to miss you guys. Let's keep in touch, okay?"

Reading a text on her cell phone, Alani brightened. "Well apparently, we will!" she said. "We've all been invited back next year to finish our projects—once they rebuild the research center."

"Great!" Billy said.

Ira looked at the fishbowl Billy carried. "Is it true

what Skull told everyone, that your little goldfish was turned into a monster?" he asked.

Billy held up Goo Fish Junior's bowl. "I can't say for sure exactly what happened. It's all a blur. But even so, I think I'm going to try a different project next time."

"I think that's a really good idea," Ira said. The others nodded in agreement.

Then they all laughed.

That was when Billy realized two familiar faces were missing. He looked back across the dock, scanning the island, until he finally spotted a sulking Bulk and Skull. They were still wearing their janitor overalls, pushing garbage cans.

"What's going on with them?" Billy asked. "Aren't they coming back?"

"Those two?" Ira said. "They will, but some of us students put in a few words and they're not allowed on the same water shuttle as the rest of us. It's pretty packed, anyway, but they're going to have to stay behind for a few days and help clean up the mess!"

Billy tried not to laugh as the two bullies passed by. The punishment did seem appropriate, though.

"All the food you can eat, *hmph*!" Bulk said,

pushing the full garbage can.

Skull cast a nervous glance at the goldfish in Billy's bowl.

"It could be worse, Bulk," Skull said. "Overeating can be a *really* bad thing."